KU-252-275

'A brilliant first novel – dark, romantic and scholarly – about the love between reader and writer, and the attraction that the mad and impossible hold for the sane and orderly'
Fay Weldon, *Sunday Times*

'It belongs to the tradition of quest stories and seeks a delineation of the relationship between writer and reader . . . Duncker raises issues about Eliot's theory of the impersonality of the artist, about the nature of madness, and about the nature of love . . . Her provocative writing is welcome'
Financial Times

'The story of a scholarly quest and a love affair, Patricia Duncker's first novel succeeds, like the narrator's nightmares, in creating an uneasy and uncomfortable environment in which questions are posed but seldom answered, and ambiguous desires are at the centre of relationships . . . The reader's and the writer's voices are left to speak without interruption, and their hopeless situation is all the more affecting'
Times Literary Supplement

'*Hallucinating Foucault* is cunning, post-modern and so forth, but one ends up believing in Duncker as a novelist for the simplest, old-fashioned reason that she has made us believe in her seething, wounded creation'
Independent

PATRICIA DUNCKER was born in the West Indies. She teaches writing, literature and feminist theory at the University of Wales and lives for part of the year in France. *Hallucinating Foucault* is her first work of fiction.

HALLUCINATING FOUCAULT

Patricia Duncker

PICADOR

For S.J.D.
my reader

First published 1996 by Serpent's Tail

This edition published 1997 by Picador
an imprint of Macmillan Publishers Ltd
25 Eccleston Place, London SW1W 9NF

Associated companies throughout the world

ISBN 0 330 35177 X

9 8 7 6 5 4 3 2 1

A CIP catalogue record for this book is available from
the British Library

Phototypeset by Intype London Ltd
Printed and bound in Great Britain by
Mackays of Chatham PLC, Chatham, Kent

ACKNOWLEDGEMENTS

This book is a work of fiction and is therefore closely based on the lives of a good many real people whom I have had the pleasure of knowing. I would like to thank the staff and patients at Sainte-Marie in Clermont-Ferrand, the real Pascal Vaury for his time and expertise, everyone at Villa Saint-Benoît, Berre-Les Alpes, including Baloo, the guardian of the gateway. I could never have written a word without the constant support, practical care and boundless generosity of Nicole Thouvenot, Jacqueline Martel and S.J.D. to whom this book is dedicated, as always, with all my love.

Patricia Duncker
France, 1995

CAMBRIDGE

THE DREAM UNFOLDS like this. I am facing a mass of hot, grey rocks, overhung by huge wedges of concrete, shaped like coffins. As I look to my left I see the glittering, undulating sea, the light catching each crest. The sea is empty. It is high summer, but there is no one there. There are no boats, no windsurfers, no parachute gliders, no swimmers, no families, no dogs. The coloured pennants in the little beach café are all aloft, full in the wind. The spray touches the barrels which support the planks of the café floor, boards pale as driftwood, smooth beneath my feet. But there is no one there. The tables are deserted. The bar is empty. The glasses are packed away. There is no one there. I feel the sun on my back. My eyes narrow to the glare.

And then I see that I am not alone. There are two of them, a man and a boy. They are squatting over the rock pools at the edge of the sea. Here where the waves rise with the tide the pools are left, full of tiny transparent crabs, green maidenhair, shellfish, old cans, fresh sand. They do not move. They are peering with terrible concentration into the pool. The boy's hand is still in the warm shallows. He is trying to catch something. The man's cigarette is motionless in his hand, the ash poised. He is concentrating hard, willing the child to succeed. They do not see me. I do not move. I feel the sun on my back. I smell the sea, the white light bursts in glory about them.

Then—and this is the only movement I ever see—the child has found what he sought, he is drawing it out of the pool. I cannot see what he has found. I see nothing, only his hand rising, the fall of his curls as he turns to the man, smiling, triumphant. And I see in the man's warm glance, the complicity of lovers, the friendship of many years, the enterprise of a life shared, work undertaken together, meetings in restaurants, in public places, an intimacy achieved, the promise of a thousand things we can give to each other when there is love, honesty and confidence between us. I do not know whose memory I have entered. This is not written in any of the books.

I begin screaming. I am shaking, hysterical, distraught. In the dream I reach out towards them, to clamp that moment back into time, to halt the corruption of change, to lock them forever into the acknowledged joy of companionship and affection, across the gulf in their lives and in mine. That glance between them gleams, frozen forever on the hot, drenched rocks. I am awake, sweating, crying, consumed by the horror of what I am unable to prevent.

Sometimes I lose my grasp on what happened in the summer of 1993. I have only these evil, recurring dreams.

I took my first degree at Cambridge. I studied French and German. In my last year I specialised in modern French, linguistics and literature. I also took a paper in modern French history. I ought to tell you that because it explains why I got so involved in the whole affair. It was already my chief interest, my intellectual passion if you like. It doesn't explain why it all became so personal. Or maybe it does. You see, when I decided to go on with my studies and to do a doctorate I was making a real commitment, not just to my writing, but to his. Writing a thesis is a lonely obsessive activity. You live inside your head, nowhere else. University libraries are like madhouses, full of people pursuing wraiths, hunches, obsessions. The person with whom you spend most of your time is the person you're writing about. Some people write about schools, groups of artists, historical trends or political tendencies. There were graduates doing that in my year, but usually one central figure emerges. In my case it was Paul Michel.

Everyone has heard of Paul Michel, with a little prompting. He wrote five novels and one collection of short stories between 1968 and 1983. His first novel, *La Fuite*, translated into English under the title *Escape* in 1970, was a set text on the modern French novel course when I was an undergraduate. He won the Prix Goncourt in 1976 with *La Maison d'Eté*, which all the critics say is his most perfect book. I wouldn't disagree. Technically, it is; and it's a book that deals with classic themes, the family, inheritance, the weight of the past. It reads like a book written by a man of seventy who has passed his life in peace and meditation. But Paul Michel wasn't like that. He was the wild boy of his generation. He made news. He was inside the Sorbonne in 1968, throwing Molotov cocktails at the CRS. He was arrested on suspicion of terrorism in 1970. And there was talk of intervention from the Elysée to have him released. Some people say he may have been a member of Action Directe. But I don't think he was. Although his public political statements were sufficiently extreme. Somehow he was never interviewed in studios or apartments as writers usually are, with their shelves of books and African statuettes behind them. I can't think of any images of him taken indoors. He is always outside, in cafés, in the street, leaning against cars, riding pillion on a motorbike, gazing at a landscape of white rock, scrub bush and umbrella pines. He was more than good-looking. He was beautiful. And he was homosexual.

He was outspokenly homosexual, I suppose. Reading through all the interviews he ever gave I noticed that he insisted on his sexuality with an aggression which was characteristic of the period. But there was no other name ever associated with his. He never had a life-time partner as some gay writers do. He was always alone. He seemed to have no family, no past, no connections. It was as if he was the author of himself, a man without kin. Some critics pointed out, patronisingly I always thought, that homosexuality was only one theme among many in his work and he could not be considered merely as a gay writer. But I did think it was central. I still do. His perspectives on the family, society, heterosexual love, war, politics, desire, were always those of an outsider, a man who has invested nothing and who therefore has nothing whatever to lose.

And I had one other clue around which to build my image of Paul Michel. In a late interview with an American review, the *New York Times Review of Books*, I think, when *Midi* was published in English, he was asked which other writer had influenced him most. And he answered without hesitation, Foucault. But he would make no further comment.

Of course, Paul Michel was a novelist and Foucault was a philosopher, but there were uncanny links between them. They were both preoccupied with marginal, muted voices. They were both captivated by the grotesque, the bizarre, the daemonic. Paul Michel took his concept of transgression straight from Foucault. But stylistically they were poles apart. Foucault's huge, dense, Baroque narratives, alive with detail, were like paintings by Hieronymous Bosch. There was an image, a conventional subject, a shape present in the picture, but the texture became vivid with extraordinary, surreal,

disturbing effects as eyes became radishes, carrots, as earthly
delights became fantasies of torture with eggshells, bolts and
ropes. Paul Michel wrote with the clarity and simplicity of
a writer who lived in a world of precise weights and absolute
colours, a world where each object deserved to be counted,
desired and loved. He saw the world whole, but from an
oblique angle. He rejected nothing. He was accused of being
atheist, unscrupulous, a man without values. His more perceptive—and hostile—critics saw him as a writer who faced
each event with the stoic indifference of an accepted destiny,
whose political commitment was no more than an existential
gesture, a man without morals or faith.

It was certainly true that his political life and his writing
life seemed to be divided by a crevasse. He was personally
involved in the radical left, but his writing addressed classical
traditions, with what could be described as an olympian
elitism. The elegance of his prose was stamped with the
highhandedness of indifference. His life was engaged with
the times, his writing was that of an aristocrat who has
owned land for centuries, who knows that his peasants are
loyal and that nothing will ever change. It was a mysterious
contradiction. It was not true of Foucault; and if I had to
choose between them as my comrade on the barricades I
would have chosen Foucault. He was the idealist; Paul
Michel was the cynic.

But writing and politics have very little to do with each
other anyway in the English tradition. Or at least they
haven't done since the demise of Winstanley and John
Milton. I didn't want to become mired in agonised liberal-
ism. I read all of E. M. Forster in my last year at school. He
had a dreadful effect upon me. I think that's why I became
so involved with the French.

I was going out with a Germanist when I began my

research on Paul Michel. She was an intense-looking woman, a bit older than I was. I first saw her going into the Rare Books Room of the University Library. She had a mass of curly brown hair and wore tiny, round, thin-rimmed glasses. She was bony and quick in her movements, skinny as a boy, oddly dated in her manners, like a mid-nineteenth-century heroine. I thought she looked fascinating. So I transported myself and all my books to the Rare Books Room.

She smoked. And that was how I got to know her. Very few of the graduates smoked, and there was a sort of prison yard next to the tea room in which the smokers walked round and round, consuming our poisons. I waited until she had finished her tea and set off round the yard. Then I followed her at a safe distance. When she had her cigarette well alight and was marching purposefully towards the magnolia I caught up with her and asked for a light. I know it's a pick-up line that must have been used by Neanderthal man, but women writing theses never usually notice that you're trying to pick them up. Ask them to tell you about their work and they'll usually do just that. For hours, without let or hindrance. So I didn't ask her what she was doing. I asked her how long she'd been doing it. Two years, she said. And she didn't volunteer any further information. I asked her where she lived. Maid's Causeway, she said. And in so final a tone I didn't feel I could go on and ask for the number. So I thanked her for the light and pushed off, feeling as crestfallen as if she'd bitten me.

Next day she walked straight up to me in the tea room and came out with an accusation that certainly didn't sound like a pick-up line.

"Why do you sit in the Rare Books Room if you're working on Paul Michel? You don't have to order any rare books."

I kept my wits about me.

"How do you know that I'm working on Paul Michel?"

"I went through your books while you were having a piss."

I was flabbergasted. She admitted to spying on me. And she was still standing there, with her curly hair in her eyes, waiting for an answer. I was so frightened of her that I told the truth.

"I work there so that I can look at you."

"I thought so," she cried vindictively.

"Am I so obvious?" We weren't even going out with each other and yet we were having our first row.

"Telling me. Have-you-got-a-light?" She mimicked my voice contemptuously. "You've been using your own cigarette lighter for the past five months."

"So you've been watching me?" I retaliated, trying to get a foothold in the conversation.

"Natch," she said, sitting down and lighting up, "only five of us in modern languages are smokers and you're one of them."

I thought she was going to put her tongue out at me. She looked like a triumphant schoolgirl who'd just won all the marbles.

"Why didn't you ask me what I do?"

She was on the offensive again. "You don't know, do you? You think all academic women are blue-stockinged bimbos."

"Hang on," I interrupted defensively. The situation had got completely out of hand. "Why are you quarrelling with me?"

"I'm not." She smiled, for the first time, a wonderful boyish grin. "I'm asking you out."

"You can't smoke that in here," snapped the woman from the cash desk, who had come up behind her. "Go outside at once."

I wolfed my cake and followed her out into the yard. I couldn't believe my luck.

"So you'd already noticed me?" I demanded, incredulous.

"Yup," she said peaceably, "have a cig. And you can use your own lighter this time."

"Look," she went on, "I live in a two-room flat, so you can't move in. But I'd like to go to bed with you. So why don't you come round tonight?"

I dropped my cigarette in a puddle. She grinned some more.

"Chicken," she hissed, her eyes glittering behind the thick lenses and silver rims. And that was how the affair between us began.

She was a very good linguist. She spoke fluent French. In her year out between public school and Cambridge she had worked as a student language teacher in a lycée outside Aix-en-Provence. She mastered schoolchildren by day and the thugs in a bar at night. She had read every single one of Paul Michel's books and had opinions, different opinions from everybody else, about each one of them. I didn't know if it was because she didn't want to tread on my toes, but it was quite hard to extract her views in detail. It was clear, however, that she had fairly ferocious ideas of her own. She also had decided ideas about what should happen between us in bed. I thought that this was absolutely wonderful as I didn't have very much to do. She was writing her thesis on Schiller. I didn't think that Schiller stood a chance.

At the beginning of an affair lovers usually spend a lot of time in bed. Even when they do manage to get up they're exhausted; worn out with achievements, victories. But this wasn't true of the Germanist. At eight o'clock she was up, with her glasses in place, busy making coffee in my kitchen or in hers. I would hear the ferocious sound of the whirling

Moulinex, smell the terrible, inevitable fumes of that strong, black, anti-aphrodisiac and know that the working day had begun. She made toast, scoured the sink, packed her bag and set off on her bicycle. Whatever the weather. By nine-thirty she had her head down in the Rare Books Room. As I say, Schiller didn't stand a chance. I used to turn up at eleven, a little giddy, still reeling with sex. She would raise her head, magnificent and censorious as a schoolmistress, and consent to twenty minutes break for coffee and a cigarette.

I loved her flat. She lived in two rooms, with a kitchen which looked out down the garden and was painted yellow and blue. Her cups were yellow and her plates were blue. She always had fresh flowers on the table. She bleached the surfaces and the sink. Her movements, when she was cooking, were intense and exact. So was her writing. When I finally managed to get up I would find brief notes left on the table.

Coffee on stove. Fresh bread in bin. Use old loaf first.

I kept every single one of these cryptic messages, as if I would one day find the key to decode them.

She used to leave messages for herself above the bathroom mirror. On that first morning when I struggled to the loo feeling like a battered piano, I saw, typed out in large block letters, emphatic, aggressive, Posa's demand for freedom to King Philip II.

SO GEBEN SIE GEDANKENFREIHEIT
(*Give us freedom of thought*)

And, like Posa, the Germanist meant it. She wanted freedom in every respect—theologically, politically, sexually. I used to write down the bathroom mirror messages, which were always in German, look up any words I didn't know and ponder their elliptical meanings.

Her other room was a startling, decadent mass of reds; a scarlet bedspread threaded with gold, an old Turkish carpet which was her father's gift, a turbulent web of ochre, brown and gold. The lampshades, adorned with hanging tassels of red lace, had escaped from a Regency brothel. She had a huge, empty birdcage, shaped like a bell jar. On her desk was a mass of paper, overrun with her precise and tiny handwriting. It seemed to me that she had enough material for a dozen theses already. I peered at her notes. I could understand nothing. Otherwise, every single surface was coated in books. She spent all her money on books and all her time reading them. They were all marked with criticisms, responses in the margins, sometimes interleafed with whole pages of commentary. She prowled across centuries of writing, leaving her mark wherever she went.

When we had been together for a month or so I took the risk of hunting for the shelf where she kept her copies of all the novels of Paul Michel. Sure enough, there they were, all together, in chronological order, amassed in a privileged position beside her desk. Each book was filled with as much of her writing as his. She had answered him, in full. There were white paper markers, pages of notes, dates marked on the inside cover, which I realised were the months in which she had read them. Unlike many other commentators on his work she preferred the later texts. She had read *La Fuite* as an undergraduate, as I had, but she had read *Midi* twice and *L'Evadé* three times. I was puzzled and pleased. I found a sheaf of her writing inside the text of Paul Michel's last novel. These referred me to particular pages, incidents, passages. There was one paragraph that she had almost defaced with her meticulous, savage handwriting. At the bottom of the page she had written in her emphatic tiny block letters, BEWARE OF FOUCAULT, as if the philosopher was a particularly savage dog. I had the same edition, so I wrote down the page number. Just beneath I noticed that she had also marked a reference to a passage in one of Foucault's interviews. I wrote that down too and decided to decipher this particular cryptic message which she had written to herself. She knew perfectly well that I was writing about Paul Michel and Foucault. Never once had she expressed an opinion on this particular relationship. Now I knew she had one, her silence seemed odd, even sinister. But she must have had her reasons for saying nothing. I was prying into her secrets. I guiltily replaced the book on the shelf.

I stood in the middle of her room, mystified. Then I scoured her entire flat for Foucault, but could not find any of his books. He had clearly been banned.

She seemed to be present in her rooms even when she was not there; the smell of her cigarettes, the cumulative effect of the incense she burned, the can of oil she kept on the window sill for her bike chain, the muddy gloves she used for gardening. I liked to sit there, trying to piece her together, as if she were a puzzle to be solved. For she didn't quite add up. On the one hand she operated with quite terrifying directness. Never before had I been told to take my trousers off while the woman watched. But on the other hand there were sides to her that were fragile, cryptic, hidden. If I touched her when she had not expected me to do so she shrank back, shaking. There were times when she was writing and I would see her covering the page briskly, then she would pause, staring into space, frozen, unmoving, for over twenty minutes, the pen perched like a bird against her cheek. I did not dare to disturb her or ask where she had been. She was like a military zone, some of it mined.

One day I came down to her flat to find her because she wasn't in the library and there she was, writing in bed, her face wet with tears. I took her in my arms and kissed her. She let me do that once, then pushed me away. I looked down at her writing and saw that it was a letter addressed to "*Mein Geliebter . . .*"—she had written pages and pages in German. I nearly had a brain haemorrhage with jealousy.

"What the fuck are you doing?" I shouted.

"Writing a love letter to Schiller."

"A what?"

"You heard."

"Are you serious?"

"Absolutely. It helps me to get a grip on him. To think clearly. If you're not in love with the subject of your thesis it'll all be very dry stuff, you know. Aren't you in love with Paul Michel?"

"No. Or at least I don't think so."

"Can't see why not. He's very good-looking. And he likes boys."

"I'm in love with you," I said.

"Don't be such an idiot," she snapped, leaping out of bed and scattering her passion for Schiller all over her Turkish rug. I tried not to treat Schiller as a serious rival, but he was. She spent more time with him than she did with me.

I come from a fairly ordinary middle-class family. My dad's a physicist and my mother's a GP. They met at college. I've got one sister who's six years younger than me. We were brought up like two only children really. I liked her and we used to play together, but we had our own friends, our own lives. The Germanist, however, came from not one broken home, but two. For a while I couldn't quite get my mind round her family circumstances. She had two fathers and her mother had apparently disappeared.

"I know it sounds weird," she said, "having two dads. But I always have had. They don't live far apart. One's in West End Lane, the other one's up the hill in Well Walk. I don't know if they had joint custody or what. I've always halved my holidays between them. My first father, if you see what I mean, the one who gave me the rug, works in the Bank of England. I don't know what he does. I have to wait for security to let him out at lunchtime and they won't let me in at all. I did ask him once, you know, what he spends his days doing, and he said, negotiating with other banks, but so gloomily I don't think he likes it much. Or it could have been a bad day on the Stock Exchange. Mother ran off with my second father when I was two and took me with her. I liked my second father a lot. He made me a huge kite with a dragon on it. He's a painter, sells masses now, and teaches studio in an art college. It was Wimbledon, now it's Harrow, or is it Middlesex? Anyway, he does vast frescoes with his students, gigantic, all along barren walls in inner city slums. Mother didn't stay long with him either. She pushed off within a year and left me behind this time."

"No, I've no idea where she went, or who with. Nor has anyone. I've never seen her since. She must have done well though. She sent me eighteen thousand pounds when I was eighteen. A thousand for each year."

"What? You're making that up."

"No joke. I own the flat in Maid's Causeway outright. It was £27,000. The Bank of England made up the rest. Why do you think I never bitch about rent? I've had it since my second year at King's. But Mother's obviously not interested in me particularly, nor my dads. They never hear from her."

"Haven't they remarried?"

"She wasn't married to either of them. Martin, that's the painter, had a girlfriend who lived with us for a couple of years, now he's got one who doesn't. And the Bank of England is homosexual. He has lots of boys. They're usually great. They all love cooking. So does Dad. We eat like lords."

I sat with my mouth open.

"Your dad's gay?"

"Yup. Like Paul Michel."

"Is that why you've read all his books so carefully?"

"I read everything carefully," she snapped witheringly.

She said nothing for a while. Then she said, "My dad's read some of Paul Michel. He reads French. It's interesting having nothing but fathers. Different if you're a man. Paul Michel was always searching for his Oedipal ogre."

"Who's that?"

"Foucault."

And that was the first time she'd mentioned his name. I couldn't ask any pointed questions without revealing that I'd been digging about in her shelves. Besides, she got up to go back to the Rare Books Room, thereby indicating that the conversation was decisively over.

That night she went to a film at the German Society which I'd already seen, so I stayed home and looked up the offending passage in *L'Evadé*. This is what Paul Michel had written.

The cats are asleep at the end of my bed and all around me, the thundery silence of L'Escarène, caught at last in the rising flood of warm air, carrying the sand from the south. The Alps are folded above in the flickering light. And on the desk in the room beneath lies the writing which insists that the only escape is through the absolute

destruction of everything you have ever known, loved, cared
for, believed in, even the shell of yourself must be discarded
with contempt; for freedom costs not less than everything,
including your generosity, self-respect, integrity,
tenderness—is that really what I wanted to say? It is what
I have said. Worse still, I have pointed out the sheer
creative joy of this ferocious destructiveness and the
liberating wonder of violence. And these are dangerous
messages for which I am no longer responsible.

It was an important message, disturbing if taken out of
context, but there were other things in *L'Evadé* which con-
tradicted this savage despair. It took me over an hour in the
library to find the interview with Foucault because it dated
from 1978, but was published posthumously in *L'Express*,
13th July 1984, and consisted of Foucault denouncing his
own work, *Les Mots et les choses*.

It is the most difficult, the most tiresome book I ever
wrote . . . madness, death, sexuality, crime—these are the
subjects that attract most of my attention. By contrast, I
have always considered *The Order of Things* to be a kind
of formal exercise.

I could see no connection whatever between the two
passages, beyond the obvious fact that Foucault's sinister list
of obsessions was an excellent summary of all the themes in
Paul Michel's fiction. I read through the entire interview.
There was only one other phrase which she had written
down, it was not even a complete sentence. It was this:

the craving, the taste, the capacity, the possibility of an
absolute sacrifice . . . without any profit whatsoever,
without any ambition.

Now I was utterly baffled and very intrigued. The extremity of this kind of language—"craving", "absolute sacrifice"—common both to Paul Michel and to Foucault, played no part in the Germanist's daily intellectual discourse. Even if she talked about her work it was often in terms of form, or of one particular poem, play or letter to Goethe. I realised that I had no sense of her overall project, only a fascinating perspective on her engagement with detail. I had no idea what she was actually doing. On the other hand, she sat me down, almost every evening, and delivered a series of questions worthy of the inquisition. She was much sharper and more aggressive than my doctoral supervisor, who gazed at my pages of typescript with weary indifference.

I became increasingly fascinated by her antipathy to Foucault.

Everybody knew her. All the graduates dreaded her appearance when they were giving papers. She had always read everything and had her own, peculiar, controversial, but well-substantiated views. Even when she stepped outside for a cigarette she still seemed to know what had happened in the seminar. She didn't have any close friends. And she had always lived alone. I lived with an English graduate called Mike who was working on Shakespeare. He was mightily intimidated by the Germanist and fell preternaturally silent whenever she arrived in our flat. I think it was her glasses. She had such thick lenses that they magnified her eyes. The result was an owl-like intensity, combined with an uncanny concentration. Somehow, you found yourself reflecting on the fact that owls ate live mammals.

"What on earth do you talk about?" Mike asked incredulously, after she had spent her first night in our flat and vanished at dawn.

"Oh, everything. Her work. My work. She's got two fathers."

"I suppose one of them is Zeus," said Mike.

She was never affectionate. She never used any terms of endearment, never told me that she loved me, and never held my hand. When she took me to bed she kissed me as if there was some distance to be covered and she was intent on getting there without interference.

It was the end of May, exam time for the undergraduates. We were all infected with exam paralysis as well as thesis paranoia. I was playing chess with Mike in our kitchen on the freshly bleached formica table from which the Germanist had eliminated all traces of stickiness, when she bounced in unannounced. This was unheard of. If she intended to come round she rang up in advance and made meticulous arrangements. If I wasn't there she left messages with Mike, which she recited at dictation speed as if he were an illiterate secretary.

"Get dressed sweetheart and put on your best glad rags. The Bank of England just rang from Saffron Walden. He'll be arriving in his Merc within the hour." She danced round the table. "And he's taking us both out to dinner."

I had never seen such uncharacteristic bumptiousness. I sat there thinking, she called me sweetheart. Mike was stunned. I thought I might soon need a blood transfusion.

The prospect of meeting your girlfriend's father, or at least one of her fathers, is very intimidating. I began to panic.

"Should I put on a tie? I haven't got a tie."

"Then you can't wear one," she said with devastating logic, through a cloud of smoke.

"I could borrow one off Mike."

"Oh, don't bother. Father doesn't care. We're students. Anyway, none of his boyfriends wear ties."

"But I'm not his boyfriend. I'm yours."

"Oh? Are you?" she said scornfully.

"You called me sweetheart," I accused.

"Did I? Slip of the tongue."

We stood on the steps of the Fitzwilliam peering down Trumpington Street in the golden evening light. Her father really did drive a sleek black Mercedes, equipped with car phone, CD player and a locking system which responded to a radar device on his car keys. If he pressed the control the car answered, even at long distance, with a hum and a click, a quick flash of the lights all round, and rested, open and waiting. I wondered if it worked round corners.

She didn't look like her father, but they had the same grin. He was about fifty, grey-haired, clean-shaven, handsome and unnervingly sinister, rather like a CIA agent in a 1960s film. He had all the trimmings, dark suit, pearl cuff-links and expensive French shirt. He got out of the car and stretched out his arms. I'd never seen her so happy. She let out a great shout of uncomplicated joy and he engulfed her in a hug. He even dislodged the glasses.

"How long can you stay?" she demanded, without introducing me.

"Just tonight." He kissed her on both cheeks, like the French do. Then turned to me.

"Now, my girl, let me take a look at this young man who has captivated my daughter."

I suddenly felt oily, coated in dandruff and spots, but I was delighted to hear this statement. I was under the impression that the Germanist didn't have any passions. She certainly hadn't appeared amenable to captivation. He shook my hand, then suddenly gave me a hug too. I was very taken aback and very pleased.

"If she doesn't give you a good time, boy, cruise on down

to us in London." He delivered his pick-up line with the same broad, mischievous grin she had lavished upon me.

"Give over, Dad. I saw him first," she giggled and poked her father in the ribs. I changed colour several times with embarrassment.

All my ideas about the Bank of England underwent a sudden and rapid transformation. The evening, depending upon your morals, went downhill from there. I now understood where my Germanist's absolute sense of licence and liberty came from. She was her father's daughter.

He took us to Brown's, and there amidst the pot-planted splendour of Butch Cassidy and the Sundance Kid he proceeded to eat like a student. We all had mushroom and Guinness pie. He ordered extra chips. She couldn't finish her baked potato and sour cream. He changed plates and ate the lot. He took a look at the wine list, shook his head sadly, and ordered two bottles of house red. He suggested that I put some extra cream on my Tarte Tatin, called for some more without waiting for a reply and then added a little to his own ice cream and apple pie. He was clearly fearless in the face of cholesterol.

She was transformed from the intense, abrasive graduate into a merry child. She chatted, giggled, told stories, wolfed chips, demanded news of her father's last boyfriend, who appeared to be the same age as she was. She was even irreverent about Schiller. He drew her out, encouraged her, teased her unmercifully and begged her to let him pay for contact lenses. He asked, with a wicked grin, if I was any good in bed, urged her to have driving lessons and choose a car. He ticked her off for smoking; then smoked half of my cigarettes. He was like a passing king, arbitrary, generous, dispensing largesse.

When we reached the cappuccinos he turned his strange grey eyes upon me and asked about Paul Michel.

"All I've read is *La Maison d'Eté*, the one which carried off the Goncourt. I suppose that gives me a false impression of his work. My daughter tells me that it's his most conventional novel."

"Yes," I agreed, "in some ways it is. I still prefer *La Fuite*, which talks about his childhood. And, well . . ." I hesitated.

"Growing up gay in rural France,' said the Bank of England, grinning. "Being homosexual isn't a taboo subject at this table. Poor lad, it must have warped him for life. He had a touch of the James Deans though, didn't he? A brutal butch version of homosexuality and we all end up doomed, damned and gorgeous. What's happened to him? I know that he was locked up in an institution for a bit. Not dead of AIDS, I hope."

"No," I said, "not as far as I know. He had a complete nervous breakdown of some kind in 1984. And he hasn't written anything since."

Suddenly I became aware of the Germanist. Midnight had struck, the pumpkin was gone and the magic was dissolved. She was glaring at me with her lenses alight, shining with fury.

"Then you don't know? You're studying his work and you don't know what they've done to him?"

"What do you mean?" I demanded, very startled.

"He's in the madhouse. Sainte-Anne in Paris. He's been there nine years. They're killing him with their drugs, day after day."

I stared at her.

"Calm down darling," said her father peacefully, looking round for the bill, "I didn't know that he was still in there."

"But you aren't writing a thesis on Paul Michel." She was

a column of accusation. I thought that she was going to hit me.

Her father leaned over and kissed her cheek, something I would never have dared to do, and said sweetly, "You make scenes at your lover in front of the restaurant, my dear, never at table. It's not the done thing."

The Germanist melted slightly, glared at me once more, then stormed off to the loo. Her father turned back to me.

"I didn't know that he'd been sectioned for good and all. That's a pity. Just being gay used to be enough to get you locked up, but I'd have thought things were more enlightened now. Might be worth investigating."

He helped himself to another of my cigarettes and then said, smiling, "If I were you I'd find out if the family had a hand in it. Families usually take it upon themselves to bump off their homos—dykes and gays—if they can do it with impunity."

I felt the need to defend myself.

"I'm not writing about his life. I'm studying his fiction."

"How can you separate the two?"

"Apart from *La Fuite* he's not an autobiographical writer."

"But his experiences—the ones he sought out for himself as well as the things that just happened—must be relevant."

"I think that's a trap. You can't interpret writing in terms of a life. It's too simple. Writing has its own rules."

The Germanist had reappeared like a magical apparition and pitched in on my side. "He's right, Dad. It'd be as if I explained away all Schiller's work in terms of his economic situation and the jobs Goethe got for him."

"But he couldn't have written anything if Goethe hadn't bailed him out. You've said that yourself."

"Yes. It's true. But it's still not the most important thing about his writing."

"Then," said her father emphatically, "why is it so important to know that Paul Michel is barking mad in some asylum in Paris?"

"Because," said the Germanist, turning her predatory eyes upon me, "if you love someone, you know where they are, what has happened to them. And you put yourself at risk to save them if you can."

It was as if she had flung a glove down on the table between us. I had a sudden awful vision of her searching for Schiller in the cobbled streets of Weimar with a phial of penicillin and saving him from the last, gasping stages of consumption.

We left her father in her flat, openly reading all her cryptic messages and peering into her files of notes.

"I try to get through the book lists she sends me," he said confidingly as she disappeared into the airing cupboard in search of towels, "but I don't have much time for reading. I got very stuck in Foucault."

"She told you to read Foucault?"

"She seems to think Foucault is as essential as Schiller," he confessed, shaking his head. "Can't think where she gets it all from. Her mother certainly wasn't an intellectual. Or not that I ever noticed."

The combination of the vanishing mother and the ubiquitous Foucault proved too much for me. I cycled home behind her in silence.

It was drizzling when we reached my house. All the lights were out. She sat cross-legged on my bed with raindrops in her curls and running down her glasses. She looked as if she was crying. We gazed ruefully at one another.

"Did you like my dad?" she asked, childish, insecure.

"I thought he was wonderful," I replied, quite sincerely.

She smiled. Then she took off her glasses, peered at me dubiously and apologised for her accusations.

"I'm sorry I was sharp," she said.

I kissed her very carefully, just in case she decided to bite me, and reached for the buttons on her shirt. I think that was the first time I made love to her rather than the other way around. She had such a hard, bony body, all ribs and hips. That night she felt brittle, fragile under my hands. I never felt that she gave herself up to me; it was more a question of giving in. Like a defeated revolutionary she abandoned her sexual barricade. Something broke within her, gently, quietly, reluctantly, and she buried her face in the hollow between my shoulder and my ear, unresisting. I was very alarmed by her unusual gentleness and talked to her quietly about nothing in particular until she fell asleep in my arms.

When I awoke next morning she had already gone, leaving an uncompromisingly Oedipal message on the kitchen table,

Gone back to Father

with which there was no arguing.

She wasn't in the library for three days after that. She had a sequence of unwritten rules about when it was permissible for me to ring or to call round. As the rules were never stated I only knew when I had breached them and she either sulked or told me to go before I had even half finished my grudging mug of coffee. I held out for one day, then rang her up. The Ansaphone told me that she was categorically unavailable and didn't suggest that I leave a message.

I said, "It's me. Where are you?" And left it at that. She didn't ring back.

I risked the telephone again on the morning of the third day. The message on the machine hadn't changed. I sat in the kitchen and gloomed at Mike.

"I think she's left me."

"Don't be so stupid," he said tartly. "If she was giving you the push she'd be the first one to come round and tell you. She'd never pass up the opportunity."

"Try to like her a little, Mike," I reproached him, very encouraged.

"You can't like women like that. Liking is too negligible an emotion. Anyway, she scares me shitless."

"Well, sometimes me too," I admitted.

Mike turned on the TV and we stared at the tiny screen. The news contained nothing but war, famine and disaster. Then the phone rang.

"Hello," she said, "I'm ringing from London."

"Oh. So that's where you were." I tried to sound cool. "I had wondered."

"I came home with Dad."

There was a pause. I didn't say anything.

"You're cross with me." She stated the fact.

"Well, yes, a bit. No, I bloody am. Why'd you just go off without leaving me a message? I haven't got your dad's number. I didn't even know you were there."

"I came down to find something for you. And I've got it. So don't be cross. I'm coming back tomorrow. I'll see you then." She rang off.

Mike looked at me pityingly, and raised his eyebrows.

"Why don't you find someone more normal?" he suggested.

I did begin to think this was good advice when she arrived in a taxi waving a 1984 copy of *Gai Pied Hebdo* with two naked men on the cover, one all sunburnt buttocks and the other with his leather trousers undone to the level of his pubic hair.

"Look. I've found it," she cried as if the buttocks were part of the map revealing the location of King Solomon's Mines.

"What?" I picked up her bag as she scrabbled through a mass of ads for sex aids, health warnings and photographs of jack-off parties.

"This." And she laid it out on the kitchen table, lighting her first cigarette triumphantly.

The article in question was a large two-page spread about Paul Michel. There were several photographs of him, clearly taken in the late 1970s from the Bernard Pivot interview for *Apostrophes*. He posed before the camera, cigarette in hand, still wearing his leather jacket over a black shirt, looking like a street fighter taking five minutes off from the struggle. Behind him was the river and the tiny model of the Statue of Liberty. He looked as if he was about to leave for America. I stared at his handsome, shut, arrogant face, the artificiality of his frozen gestures, the chill self-confidence with which he had invented himself. Then I looked at the article: *Paul Michel: L'Epreuve d'un écrivain.*

"Read it," she said. "I won't say anything."

I looked at her. She returned my glance steadily. Then I realised that this was the glove on the table. This was the obscure challenge, a demand, the first demand she had ever made upon me. I took a deep breath, sat down at the kitchen table and began to read.

PAUL MICHEL
L'Epreuve d'un écrivain

On the night of 30 June 1984 Paul Michel was
arrested in the graveyard at Père Lachaise. He was
found screaming and crying, overturning tombstones
with a crowbar. The cemetery watchman, M. Jules
Lafarge, tried to stop him, whereupon the writer
attacked the watchman, fracturing his skull with the
crowbar which he subsequently used to break M.
Lafarge's forearm and to inflict multiple injuries on his
back and face. Paul Michel, described as incoherent
and dangerous by the SAMU officials who eventually
managed to control him, was admitted to the psychiatric unit at Sainte-Anne a few days later. He has been
diagnosed as suffering from paranoid schizophrenia. It
was later revealed that the writer had escaped from the
restraints placed upon him in the hospital and had
slashed his chest several times with a razor stolen from
one of the other patients. He is not thought to be in
any danger.

The heterosexual press have not hesitated to specu-
late on the supposed connection between Paul Michel's
madness and his homosexuality. But who is Paul
Michel? The identity of a writer is always a subject for
speculation. Writing is a secret art; a hidden, coded
practice, often carried out in darkness behind locked
doors. The process of making writing is an invisible
act. Paul Michel suggested this link between writing
and homosexual desire.

Fiction, he said, was beautiful, unauthentic and useless, a profoundly unnatural art, designed purely for
pleasure. He described the writing of fiction, telling
stories, telling lies, as a strange obsession, a compulsive
habit. He saw his own homosexuality in similar terms;

as a quality that was at once beautiful and useless, the potentially perfect pleasure.

Throughout his years as a militant gay activist Paul Michel always insisted on the controversial view that we are not born comme ça, but choose to be so. This brought him into sharp conflict with the religious association for homosexual rights, David and Jonathan, who have always argued for tolerance, comprehension and the extension of civil liberties to lesbians and gay men on the grounds that homosexuality is the result of an innate biological determinism. The politically convenient aspect of this theory is of course the fact that homosexuals cannot therefore be held responsible for what is their natural condition. No one can be blamed. Paul Michel was defiantly against nature. To be unnatural, he argued, was to be civilised, to stake one's claim to an intellectual self-consciousness which was the only foundation for making art. He relished the improbable, bizarre aspects of gay life; he frequented the leather bars, the drag shows, the baths, the roughest cruising grounds. He resisted every tendency within the community which argued for an extension of bourgeois privilege to lesbians and gays and was perversely opposed to the Partenairiat scheme which would have accorded social security, tenancy and pension rights to established gay couples. He was contemptuously dismissive of the efforts of the parliamentary socialist group, Gaies pour les libertés. He cherished the role of sexual outlaw, monster, pervert. So far as we know he never lived within a stable partnership. He was always alone.

Out of this eerie mixture of defiant difference and sincere commitment to the collective struggle of the gay community in our efforts to win recognition and the right to exist, comes Paul Michel's writing, classi-

cal, detached, austere. This is a writing which refuses
the decadent excess of his sexual life and his political
extremism. His most recent novel, *L'Evadé*, is a haunt-
ing story of flight and pursuit, a terrifying tale of adventure and escape, the sufferings of his unnamed narrator
are as gripping and as poignant as those of Jean Valjean.
Yet this text is also a psychic journey to the edge of
experience, a modern parable of exploration through
the dark labyrinth of the soul. His work was of that
uncanny quality which ensured recognition from a
usually hostile literary establishment. He was their
scandal, their exception, their prodigal son. Paul
Michel used his fame and the frequent opportunities
he had to hold court in public to promote his version
of homosexuality, but with ambiguous results. He was
often deliberately antagonistic to sympathetic would-be
supporters; he took up extremely provocative political
positions, presenting gay men as a subversive vanguard
in the struggle to undermine the bourgeois state. His
public discourse was that of a man at war, against
society certainly, and, we suspect, against himself.

One of the clearest influences upon his work was
that of the philosopher, Michel Foucault. Paul Michel
insists that the two writers never met. We think that
this is improbable given that during the student unrest
of 1971 the two of them were recorded on film,
crouched side by side, flinging roof tiles at the police
from the top of one of the besieged university buildings
at Vincennes. Foucault's only known comment on the
work of Paul Michel was published in this review
(October 1983), where he described the novelist as
"beautiful, excessive and infuriating". Foucault
pointed out the elegance and restraint of the writing as
opposed to the peculiarly lurid exaggerations of Paul
Michel's political statements. When asked to comment

further on this apparent contradiction, Foucault was typically enigmatic. "What contradiction? Excess is essential to the production of austerity. Paul Michel is dedicated to his profession. That's all."

Nevertheless, the two writers explored similar themes: death, sexuality, crime, madness, an irony now all too evident as we contemplate the recent tragic death of Michel Foucault and the terrible fate of Paul Michel. Paul Michel last appeared in public at the ceremony held in the courtyard of the Hôpital de la Salpêtrière as Foucault's body was removed on its last journey south to Poitiers where he was buried. The ceremony was attended by many of Foucault's famous colleagues and friends. Paul Michel read from the philosopher's work, including the following passage from Foucault's Preface to *La Volonté de Savoir*, which struck us to be of particular significance.

There are times in life when the question of knowing if one can think differently than one thinks and perceive differently than one sees is absolutely necessary if one is to go on looking and reflecting at all.

People will say, perhaps, that these games with oneself need only go on behind the scenes; that they are, at best, part of those labours of preparation that efface themselves when they have had their effects. But what, then, is philosophy today—philosophical activity, I mean—if not the critical labour of thought upon itself? And if it does not consist, in place of legitimating what one already knows, in undertaking to know how, and up to what limit, it would be possible to think differently?

For this perilous enterprise, the revolutionary project of thinking differently, was at the core of Foucault's philosophy and the fiction of Paul Michel.

Paul Michel's courage has never been disputed.

Whatever we feel concerning the provocative extremity of his behaviour and the ways in which he chose to shape his life, it is undeniable that he was never afraid to put himself at risk. Extremity is not necessarily madness. But the forms which madness takes are never without significance. What then is the significance of his behaviour in the graveyard? A writer plays many parts, becomes many people in the course of his creative life. The part which Paul Michel is playing now cannot have been chosen. We are in danger of losing one of our finest writers to the white prison walls of a psychiatric unit, to the very institutional forces that both he and Foucault have put so radically in question.

Christian Gonnard

I put down the copy of *Gai Pied Hebdo* and stared at her.

"Do you think he was really that violent?" she asked, her face blank, speculative, watching me.

"You don't imagine fractured skulls or gaping razor slashes across your chest."

"What will you do?" Her cigarette hung in mid-air. I suddenly realised that if I gave the wrong answer she would abandon me then and there. But the sinister fact was that I already knew the right answer. The words were forming—practical, mad—waiting to be spoken.

"I'll go to Paris," I said. "My father promised that he'd fund a Paris trip to look at the letters. They're deposited either in the Centre Michel Foucault or in the university Library Archive. I'll find out where Paul Michel is. After all, we know he's not dead, but we can't be sure he's still in Sainte-Anne."

Her cigarette had not moved. I took a deep breath and

snatched up the gage she had flung down in my path. It was as if the formica buckled on the kitchen table.

"If I can—if he's well enough—I'll get him out."

She stubbed out the butt with murderous intensity and looked up at me. I was shaking.

"I love you," she said.

I collapsed on to the table with my head in my hands. She got up at once. By the time I had summoned the courage to raise my head she had gone. The outer door banged behind her. Mike was standing beside me, his face all anxiety and concern.

"Are you all right?" He put his arm around my shoulders. "Shall I make some tea? She's gone."

"I know," I gulped.

"Was it dreadful?"

"Yes."

"Did she break it off?" He turned on the tap and ran a fountain of cold water down the kettle's spout.

"No. Or at least I don't know. She may have done. She told me she loved me."

Mike dropped the kettle in the sink.

It was June. The exams were over and the undergraduates were recovering from their hangovers. All the courtyards in Cambridge sprouted large cream tents and duckboards, an elegant parody of the First World War landscapes. I asked the Germanist if she had ever been to a May ball. She simply stared at me with undisguised contempt. So I sold the tickets and wrote to my father asking for the money to go to Paris. He replied warmly, mentioning vast sums. They loved telling their friends that their son was studying at Cambridge and realised that such boasts never came cheaply.

The tiny, white stone city on the edge of the Fens had

seemed intensely romantic when I first came up as an undergraduate. It was like Gawain's castle, a shimmering mass of
pinnacles, an intimate world of friendships on staircases. I
loved the smell of the libraries, the river weeds, the cut grass
in summer. But staying on as a graduate changed my images
of the city. A new geography emerged, one based on our flat
off Mill Road, the supermarket, the local junk store, run by
an enormous family, that sold kitchen rolls, plastic buckets
and washing-up brushes at Third World prices. I noticed the
wind, that slicing white wind, which comes straight from
the Urals, for the first time. I began to stare at the waste
paper blowing across Parker's Piece. I got depressed in the
evenings. Maybe the first year of a research project is always
a tunnel of disillusionment. Once freed from the appalling
task of thinking through eight or ten weekly sides of not
very original, turgid prose I had imagined that the gates of
scholarship would roll open before me, as if I had just
acquired an extensive country estate. No one ever pointed
out that research would be a dull, confusing, depressing,
endless chore. I had no sense of direction. My supervisor
would occasionally suggest that I read such and such a book,
article or unpublished thesis. The other theses were the most
devastating experience I have ever had. It is no small task
to convert unique, extraordinary passions into pages of
reductive, repetitive commentary. The worst one I read was
a comparative study of Paul Michel and Virginia Woolf.

The producer of this thesis was a graduate from Oxford.
He argued that both Paul Michel and Virginia Woolf were
essentially Romantics, that their method was Romantic, that
their epiphanies were revelatory moments of being. He
maintained that their preoccupations with inner landscapes
represented a disillusionment with politics and a Romantic
affirmation of the inward life of the soul. He ground out

page after page and acres of footnotes, citations, cross-references, all remorselessly proving this hypothesis. Paul Michel read English. But he never claimed to have read Virginia Woolf. My first moment of radical doubt came when I realised that, during the years when both writers were supposedly writhing with reclusive egotism and fanning the fires of their tortured souls, Virginia Woolf was lecturing on socialism to the women's co-operative guild and Paul Michel was part of a revolutionary Maoist cell. But the Oxford wizard wrote remorselessly on about their lack of political commitment. This was a world without inconvenient contradictions. I read every word of this thesis and emerged in need of therapy. My Germanist was unsympathetic.

"You should skim read stuff like that," she snapped, "and photocopy the bibliography."

"But it looked so scholarly," I wailed.

"You're as naïve as Dorothea."

"Who's Dorothea?"

"Read *Middlemarch*." The reply came back like a round from her machine gun.

And so the project of a doctorate diminished in grandeur before me. So too did the vain little city and its tortuous, complacent or resentful inhabitants. Cambridge became a market town of provincial proportions with an indifferent theatre, too few cinemas and too many booming, middle-class voices.

But another change had begun. I had accepted the Germanist's challenge, obscure, imprecise, inarticulate; and she stood like an image of the wind at the harbour's rim, where the calm water touched the quaking sea. She was sending me forth on an adventure. I was not going to write a mean-spirited, critical little study of a great writer. I was not going to sit in the Rare Books Room counting angels and

swallowing camels. I was going on a voyage, beyond the
damp beach of footnotes and appendices. I re-read Paul
Michel's work, breathless with excitement. I pinned a huge
poster to the kitchen wall, so that his face, steady, unsmiling,
remote, dominated our cooking. Mike thought I was mad.
He blamed the Germanist. But she was the huge swell
beneath me, the extraordinary energy itself, for all my under-
takings. She became gentler, more manageable. She began
to listen to my complaints for a few more minutes than she
usually did before biting my head off. I once found her gazing
at me, reflectively, peacefully, as if I were a painting she had
just completed.

I chose that minute to ask her about Foucault. She had
too savage a manner for pretence, so I dared the question
that had haunted me for months. What, in her opinion, was
the importance of Foucault for a man like Paul Michel? I
tried to sound casual, indifferent. She lit another cigarette
and settled herself down into her red room.

"I suggested that he was like a father, didn't I? I've thought
about that. It's true in some ways. There is almost twenty
years difference between them. For Paul Michel, Foucault
was the most important radical thinker of his times. He
belonged to the generation who rejected Sartre. They were
against the values of godless liberal humanism. They were
more extreme. But the Oedipal model doesn't really work,
does it? Paul Michel never envied Foucault; he was never
the ogre to be envied and slain. He was the beloved, the
unseen reader to be courted. I think that Paul Michel wrote
every book for Foucault. For him and against him."

I stared at her. She had pondered on the central questions
of my enquiry. She had followed me, step for step.

"Every writer has a Muse," said the Germanist slowly, "no
matter how anti-Romantic they are. For the irredeemably

boring the Muse is a woman they've cooked up in their heads, propped up like a voodoo doll on a pedestal and then persecuted with illusions, obsessions and fantasies. Paul Michel wasn't like that. He wanted someone real; someone who challenged him, but whose passions were the same. He fell in love with Foucault. It is absolutely essential to fall in love with your Muse. For most writers the beloved reader and the Muse are the same person. They should be."

She paused.

"In the case of Paul Michel this necessary love proved to be a dangerous affair."

"Why?"

"He's in an asylum, isn't he?"

I didn't understand her and my face must have registered the fact.

"Don't be so dense. Foucault was dead. For Paul Michel it was the end of writing. His reader was dead. That's why he attacked the gravestones. To dig his writing back up, out of the grave. Why bother to exist if your reader is dead? He had nothing to lose."

I whistled incredulously.

"How do you know all that? You've made it all up."

She looked at me steadily.

"Have I? Go to Paris. Find Paul Michel and ask him."

There was a heat wave at the beginning of July. The boys selling ice-cream and cold drinks became millionaires. I bought my ticket for Paris and booked myself into one of the student residences near the Porte d'Orléans. On the first Sunday morning of July the temperature was over thirty degrees in the garden by ten o'clock in the morning. I had stayed over at her flat and we lay comatose on the floor of her room, drinking iced orange juice and gazing at the

papers. I told her when I was leaving. I would be gone for
two months at least. She simply nodded and went on reading
the reviews.

"Will you miss me?" I sounded more importunate and
desperate than I had intended.

"Yes," she said, without looking up.

I sat, biting back my reply. She turned to stare at me. I
had never commented on her unexpected declaration. Neither had she.

Some lovers chat like old friends when they are making
love, keep each other informed, as if they were engaged
upon a common house purchase. For others making love
is their language; their bodies articulate themselves into
adjectives and verbs. For us it was the conjunction of the
mind and opposition of the stars. She transformed me, word-
lessly, into a mass of sensations, resolved me, like a symphony, into a crescendo of major chords. But she never told
me how she felt, never counted the ways in which she
loved me, nor did she ever ask my opinion or ever enquire
after any of my desires. She watched herself, and me, from
a terrible, uncompromising distance.

"What's the matter?" she asked crisply.

"Nothing. Just . . . well, I shall miss you dreadfully."

"That's good," she glittered, paused. Then she said,
"Listen, you have something very important to do. Nothing
must distract you. I've made some arrangements. You are
flying out on Thursday. Right . . . well, we'll go down to
London tomorrow night. We'll stay with my father. There's
a friend of his you'd find helpful. Someone you must meet."

I felt like a spy, receiving orders for an operation abroad.
I felt panic-stricken.

"How am I going to find Paul Michel? It's mad, all this."

"We start with the article. The Paris telephone directories

are all in the university catalogue room. We'll ring up the hospital tomorrow."

The Catalogue Room was a huge, ornate, oblong structure like a 1930s mausoleum. It was a mass of still, foetid air, smelling of fingered books and carpet cleaner. I thought that the directories might be on microfiche, but they weren't. There they stood, row upon row of massive, yellow doorstops, buried in the French section, containing all the public numbers. We looked up Sainte-Anne under "H" and found an entire page of numbers listing every service, but not the Psychiatric Service. We wrote down the central reception number. The directories let out an evil thump as we shoved them back into place. The Germanist tugged on my arm.

"Come downstairs," she hissed.

We packed ourselves into the telephone box at the bottom of the stairs. She produced a dozen £1 coins. I had a terrible sense of vertigo. She tapped out 010.33.1.45.65.80.00 without looking at the torn slip of paper, and without hesitating over the code, as if it were a number she already knew. She passed the phone to me just in time to hear an even French voice declaring that I had reached the hospital exchange. I asked for the Psychiatric Service. "Ne quittez pas," she said. The box swallowed down one coin while I was waiting. The Germanist, her ear pressed against the receiver, calmly poured in another piece of gold. Another woman's voice came on the line. I plunged in. I asked for "l'écrivain Paul Michel".

"C'est qui à l'appareil?" The voice was suspicious.

"I'm a student," I confessed, "I'm writing a thesis on Paul Michel." The Germanist kicked me in the thigh.

"Don't give everything away," she hissed.

"I'm very sorry," snapped the French voice. "I'm unable

to answer any questions whatsoever. Please refer all your enquiries to his legal representative."

"Who is that?" I asked pathetically.

She rang off.

The Germanist was jubilant. I couldn't understand her triumphant dance.

"We know all we need to know," she said. "He's there. If he wasn't she'd have said so. And they don't let anyone speak to him. All you have to do is get inside."

"Well, that mightn't be easy. What if they won't let me?"

"Now you have to find out who his legal representative is. And you have to ring up his dad. What's his father's name?"

"Michel. What else? He lives in Toulouse."

But there were three pages of Michels in the Toulouse directory.

"Never mind," she said, "you'll find it easier on the spot."

I wasn't so sure.

We rang her father from Liverpool Street. I could hear his voice, coming through loud and clear, as if he were a ventriloquist.

"Take a taxi, sweetheart. I'll give you £10 when you get here."

"Nonsense, Dad. We'll get the tube."

"You adore slumming it, don't you my love? Suit yourselves. The Chablis is in the cooler and I'm cooking up a storm for my favourite girl. Come on home. I hope your heart still belongs to Daddy."

"Leave off, sexy," she giggled.

He teased her with every insinuating cliché ever written. She gleamed like a wet stone under the wash of his love. They were like boxers, sparring partners, dancing, daring, testing one another's reach. I leaned against the phone box, nursing a jealous erection.

Going up in the lift at Hampstead she braced her back against the antique grille and shut her eyes. Her face looked suddenly white, fragile, child-like. I gazed at her pale skin, her scrawny body and her bare arms, now reddening from the July heat.

"You all right?" I put my chin on her shoulder.

"Yes. But I've left my womb at the bottom of the shaft," she said.

I drew back, startled, and peered at the only other occupant of the lift, a young black man on clanking roller skates with a green baseball cap pulled on backwards. His Walkman thumped gently in the hollow space. He was staring at her fixedly. As the lift arrived she opened her eyes with a snap. And behind her glasses, her eyes, vast, grey-blue, accusing, settled on the black man. The lift disgorged us into the street. She smiled, her huge, uninhibited grin. He smiled back and they slapped hands like comrades in the ghetto, boys in the hood. He rollerskated away down the hill.

"Did you know him?"

"No."

I gave up.

The house was all verticals: high windows, perpendicular bookcases, a vertiginous staircase with a steep, curving banister, an elongated umbrella-stand framing a tall, Gothic mirror. She let us in with her own key and shouted up the staircase. I had the impression that her voice rose up and up into the fragrant heights. The smell was bay leaves, cinnamon and red wine, winter smells in a summer season.

The Bank of England swung down the staircase like an extra on the set of *Billy Budd* and caught us both up, one in each arm.

"Mes enfants," he cried, and kissed whatever was in reach.

"You handsome young rogue," he laughed and patted my cheek. "I'm as crazy about you as she is. Come on upstairs. Jacques is here and can't wait to discuss diseases. That's his thing, you know," he said confidingly to me, "madmen and murderers. Well, whatever turns you on. I'm very liberal."

The kitchen and living room took up all the second floor and was the same blend of warm reds as her bed-sitting room. A gigantic African tapestry hung on one wall. There was a colossal musical engine in one corner which looked as if it had been stolen from Jean-Michel Jarre, with speakers like vertical black tombstones. Mercifully, it wasn't in operation. Coiled up on the caramel sofa, amid a mass of red and orange cushions, was the tallest man I had ever seen. He uncoiled to well over two metres and then stooped to shake hands.

"How do you do? I am Jacques Martel."

His hair was grey, but his age was unguessable. His face narrowed to a point like that of a weasel, and as he smiled two long lines appeared on either side of a sinister, professional grimace. His breath smelled of alcohol and cigarettes. He stood so close to me that I noticed his teeth. They were all slightly sharpened into points, suggesting the jaws of a shark.

He kissed the Germanist and said mildly, "Alors, ma fille . . . Comment vas-tu?"

Then he sat down again to stare at me. I stared back, uneasy and intrigued, wondering where to put my hands. The Bank of England organised us all into cut crystal glasses, whisky and peanuts, then dragged his daughter off to cheer him on amid his spices and soufflés. Two huge double doors opened on to the kitchen and I could hear her saying, "I've got no idea, Dad. What does it say in Delia Smith? Why not let me do the vinaigrette?" The predatory coil on the sofa completed his stare and began to ask questions. His English was faultless and without any trace of an accent. I found this most peculiar as French intonation almost always betrays native speakers.

"So . . . I'm told that you are working on Paul Michel? He was a tragic case. I've met him. Several times, in fact. I never treated him. But one of my colleagues was responsible for him in the initial stages. The affair caused a scandal at the time. It was widely discussed. And there was a fair amount of protest from his friends at *Gai Pied Hebdo*. One of the editors argued that we were trying to cure him of his homosexuality. That was nonsense. Really. He was barking mad. A typical example of the disease in some ways."

"The article I read said that he was a paranoid schizophrenic. Can you suddenly become one?"

The doctor laughed.

"No, no. Or at least I don't think so." He hesitated. Then he began to explain.

"It's very rare that you find two schizophrenics who resemble each other. The symptoms vary a great deal. Paul Michel was very disturbed, very violent. That's not unusual. But it will usually be random violence. They aren't murderers. They don't set out to kill anybody, plan it, do it. That's rare. When they're in crisis they can enact a sort of fusion with someone else close to them, love or hate, either way. They may fall in love with you. They may even take you in their arms with a passion—with a tenderness that's startling. Or they're capable of killing you. It's a terrible disease. I'm one of those doctors who think that it is a disease. You have no idea how they suffer. I can remember Paul Michel, right at the beginning. He was a very handsome man. You know that. Well, his pupils were gigantic that night when they brought him into Sainte-Anne. I was on duty. When they're in crisis the pupil can take over the whole eye. He was completely unaware of his actions. He was very violent, possessed by an extraordinary strength— quite insane."

"Do you . . . um, lock them up?" I paused. "Or tie them up?"

I had an uncanny sensation, as if Paul Michel, like a sudden dry wind, was coming closer and closer. Jacques Martel offered me a cigarette. He paused and we smoked in silence for a moment. Then he said, "Well, when I first entered the service, over twenty years ago, we did lock them up. And we really did use straitjackets. The beds in the rooms were screwed to the floors. We had guards on the wards. It was pretty brutal. And frightening. The mad- house wasn't a pleasant place. It was oppressive to both the staff and the patients. And we had bars on all the windows. Now we use drugs. But it boils down to the same thing in the end. We call them 'neuroleptiques'. I'm not sure what the word would be in English. The drugs put a straitjacket on the personality of the schizophrenic. The drugs curtail their suffering, but turn them into zombies. And their personalities degenerate. I hated watching that happen. Some of my patients would be with us for decades. Gradually they lose all their faculties. Eventually they become vegetables." He sighed. "I think that's one of the reasons I moved house. Changed direction a little."

"What do you do now?" I asked anxiously.

"I work in the prison service. I'm a consultant psychiatrist for the government. So you did hear her father right. Madmen and murderers. That's my thing." He laughed.

"Are many of your prisoners mad?"

I could smell garlic frying in the kitchen.

"Mmmmm. Most of them are disturbed. But that's some-times a result of being locked up in prison."

"Are they all murderers?" I was fascinated.

"I deal with quite a few murderers. But you mustn't have romantic ideas about them. Murderers are ordinary people." Jacques Martel smiled at me calmly. I watched the points on his teeth and shivered. The ice cubes clinked as they melted into my whisky. "But to return to Paul Michel. It didn't come upon him suddenly you know. It never does. We know very little about what causes schizophrenia, but there are patterns. All schizophrenics will have, as one of their first symptoms, what we call a 'bouffée délirante aiguë' . . ." His French suddenly sounded like a language he had learned and not his mother-tongue, ". . . this will happen when the subject is nineteen, twenty, rarely after the age of twenty-five."

"What is it? It sounds horrible," asked my Germanist. She had her arms round my neck. She smelt of onions and vinegar.

"Well, it's like a storm. A thunderstorm of madness. It just seizes the personality in its fist. They go off their heads. They may be violent, obsessive, wild. In the case of Paul Michel his lunacy was somewhat subsumed under the rubric of contemporary politics. He went quite mad in 1968."

We all laughed. The Bank of England stood in the door-way. He was wearing a wonderful plastic apron with a pink pig's head across his chest and a huge yellow slogan:

TODAY'S MALE CHAUVINIST PIG IS
TOMORROW'S BACON

"And you'll never guess who gave me this for Christmas."

He did a little dance. His daughter took his hand and pirouetted into his arms.

"Nineteen sixty-eight—Dad, just think. Wasn't it very romantic for you and Jacques?"

The doctor laughed.

"Ah, yes. So it was. Riots on the boulevards. Then we'd dash back to my apartment, all tanked up on beer and revolution, to screw each other senseless."

I felt the carpet move under my feet.

"All very fluid in those days," said the Bank of England, addressing himself to me by way of explanation. "I met her mother two years later and went for a walk on the wild side."

"You mean the other side," she giggled, kissing him. "I'm glad you did. But go on, Jacques. Don't lose the thread. What happened to Paul Michel? And how do you know about it?"

"It's all in his dossier. All the reports. Funny thing is of course nobody really noticed while the revolution was in full swing. He was wild, fairly violent, drunk, talked non-stop. But so did everybody else. He attacked a policeman. That wasn't unusual. Who didn't? Your father and I pinned one down under his riot shield and sat on him. We had to run for our lives after that. Do you remember?"

He looked straight at her father. They exchanged glances and it was then that I realised they were still lovers, twenty-five years later, and that they could lean on their memories, a secure, tried rope across the abyss.

"I do remember," said the Bank of England dreamily, rocking his daughter in his arms. Something hissed in the kitchen. They both turned and fled, leaving me to face the doctor alone. He lit another cigarette.

"Paul Michel was an extraordinary man. All schizophrenics are extraordinary. They are incapable of loving. Did you know that? Of really loving. They aren't like us. They are usually very perceptive. It's uncanny. They have a human dimension that is beyond the banality of ordinary human beings. They can't love you as another person would do. But they can love you with a love that is beyond human love. They have flashes, visions, moments of dramatic clarity, insight. They are incapable of cherishing a grudge or of planning vengeance."

Suddenly he looked at me very intently, his eyes widening.

"Listen," he said, "I have the sense of my littleness before them. We are of no consequence. *Tellement ils sont grands.*"

We sat in silence for a while, listening to the bubbling crashes in the kitchen. He went on, with the same peculiar intensity.

"They are a people who are excessively egotistical. They are also beyond egotism. They are like animals. They know who doesn't love them. They are very intuitive. And in that they are always right. They preserve themselves against evil. Instinctively, wonderfully."

He paused. "Paul Michel is like that. It was the source of his writing."

I stared at the lines on his face.

"You must remember. I have warned you. They cannot love as we do. You could say to one of them—your mother is dead. And they wouldn't react. It would mean nothing. Even without the drugs."

"Do the drugs change their personalities?" I asked anxiously. Paul Michel now seemed horrifyingly close, an ambiguous, towering, indifferent presence, like a colossus, against whom I weighed nothing.

"Yes," said Jacques Martel heavily, "they do. We adapt the dose according to the person and the gravity of their illness. We work out a regular dose. They have an injection once a month. But after ten or fifteen years . . ."

He shrugged his shoulders.

"Yes. They are transformed. They lose all sexual desire, all sense of themselves."

Then he said fiercely, "They sometimes do as he did. They refuse to take the treatment. They prefer their suffering."

I took a deep breath.

"Then he's still there. Who he is, I mean. But mad."

Jacques Martel nodded.

"He has no legal rights. He has an administrative trustee. The system in France is called 'la tutelle'. There's always a legal representative. Someone who takes care of their property, possessions, money, papers. It is someone who does this voluntarily, a 'bénévole'. There's an association. They are usually people with some sort of status in the community: priests, doctors, retired headmasters. They don't get paid to do it. Just their expenses."

"Would I need his permission? Or hers, it could be, I suppose. To go and see Paul Michel?" I asked suddenly. The moment was electric, but I could not understand why.

"No. Why should you? He's not a prisoner. You are going to see him then?" Jacques Martel's eyes never left my face. "You've decided to go?"

"I'm flying out to Paris on Thursday."

He let out his breath quietly.

"Ah . . . good," he said. It was the right answer.

"Dinner's ready. It's delicious." The Germanist danced in and embraced me. One of her curls caught across my mouth. She kissed me and took back her curl.

"Come and eat," she said.

The table was laid out in red and white, like a gladiator's feast.

She came down to Heathrow on the tube to wave me off. I sat next to her, a little quiet and sad, clutching my bags. My parents had asked to meet her. She refused point-blank, without giving a reason. All her affection, which had bubbled so encouragingly and unexpectedly during the past weeks, appeared to evaporate. She was tense, preoccupied, alert. I watched her disengaging a trolley from the long line of attached metal L-shapes, which stretched before the automatic doors like a fence across the prairie, with a sharp flick of her boot. We wandered aimlessly across the concourse, gazing up at the turning panels. My flight was on the board, but had not been called. She stacked my bags deftly on to the conveyor belt at the check-in. It was then that I noticed how strong she was. The narrow shoulders and light build that made her look so fragile beneath the black jacket and jeans were illusory. I stared at her, seeing a stranger all over again. The owl eyes turned upon me.

"I'm going to buy you an orange juice," she said. "It's hot. Fresh orange is better than chemicals."

And away she strode.

Just as the flight was called she turned to me and took my hand.

"It's only two months," I said, "two and a bit." But I said this to comfort myself. I was by now quite convinced that she wouldn't have cared if I never came back. "I'll write. Will you?"

"Yes, of course I'll write to you. Good luck. And don't lose sight of what you have gone out to do. Promise me that."

She hovered like a giant, white-faced bird, her eyes magnified, golden.

"I promise."

She kissed me once, not on my lips, but on my neck, just

below my ear. A long shiver went through me, as if I had been scratched. Then she took my arm and marched me away through the shining window frame of the metal detectors. As I passed the threshold into Departures I had one last glimpse of her, unsmiling, watching. She didn't wave. She simply watched me go. I sat down on a plastic chair and cried silently, like a bereaved child, for the next twenty minutes.

PARIS

MY MEMORIES OF those first days in Paris are like a sequence of postmodern photographs. I see the patterned metal grilles round the base of the trees on the boulevards. I see the axes of the city unfolding in one long glimmering line of bobbed trees and massive symmetrical buildings. I smell the water rushing in the gutters, hear the rhythmical swish of the plastic brooms, shaped like witches' sticks, as the street cleaners pass in luminous green. The streets stank of Gauloises and urine. I lived on pizza slices and Coca Cola. I trod in dog shit and fag ends.

My room was on the fifth floor of a student residence in the eleventh arrondissement. It had cracked cream walls and a stained basin. The vomit green lino had been carefully tortured with cigarette burns. It smelt of musty trainers and bleach. I amassed all my books, papers and courage and then went out to waste good money on a poster and a pot plant as suicide preventatives. There was an American summer school from Texas installed at the other end of the corridor. They divided into two sexes, but looked like clones, for they were all massive, blonde, sunburnt and cheerful.

On Sunday morning I walked straight through the Marais peering into the windows of incredibly expensive antique shops and came out on the rue de Rivoli. I watched the sun making long straight lines on grey stone, the waiters in floor-length white aprons sweeping out the bars and taking the chairs down from the tables. Some of the shops were open, shirts and cheap jewellery stretched out on the pavements. I picked my way past a mass of empty birdcages. In the window a flotilla of tropical fish in an illuminated tank circulated miserably, suspended in long flights of bubbles. They stared stupidly out through thick glass. I stared back, equally trapped and wretched. I had no idea where I was going. The traffic gathered heat and force. By ten o'clock it was already nearly thirty degrees under the awnings.

I crossed into a white block of sun, passed a battered builder's hoarding and found myself facing the glittering black triangles of the Pyramids in the courtyard of the Louvre. The gravel was swept carefully clean of rubbish. Tourists peered down into the galleries below. The new entrance had not been completed when I had last been in Paris. I stared at the sinister pointed shapes. As I stood before the largest of the triangles the shape began to make sense, hardened into the form of my promise to her. I was facing a prism that remained masked and simply reflected rather than refracted the light. I found myself at the base point of two interlocking triangles. It was then that I had the peculiar sensation that something was being shown to me, explained, but that I had as yet no way of breaking into the code, no means of understanding the blank, flat surfaces. It was like seeing a new language written down for the first time. I stood watching a sign that would not yield up its meaning. I remember this because it had seemed uncanny at the time.

I turned away and walked down to the quays.

Two tramps were sitting on the steps, clutching one full bottle of red wine between them and talking very seriously. As I picked my way past them they let out a series of muffled grunts. I turned and looked into their faces. One of them, despite his red, troubled forehead, was clearly a young man; he was not much older than I was. They stared back. I walked away down the warm stones, peering into the grey water, searching for an empty patch of shade. High above me the traffic soared past. Finally, I found a corner on the island, looking out towards the Pont des Arts, now reopened, repainted, rebuilt. Just out of range, as I cowered inside the shadow of swaying green, the sun turned the paving stones into a thick wash of savage white light. I sat down to read Paul Michel.

I don't know if it was the heat, the loneliness, the odd sensation of being alone with him in that huge, tourist-infested city, or the peculiar awareness of having been chosen for reasons I did not understand, but that day, for the first time, I heard the writer who was still there, even across the great desert of his insanity, even through the remote serenity of his prose. I heard a voice, perfectly coherent and clear, that whispered terrifying things.

Paul Michel had lived at risk. He had never owned property. He had never had a proper job. He lived in small rooms and high places. He searched through the streets, the cafés, the bars, the gardens of Paris: along the canals, beneath the motorways, by the river, in libraries, galleries, urinals. He moved on, from room to room, a ceaseless, unending stream of different addresses. He owned very few books. He lived out of suitcases. He smoked nearly fifty cigarettes a day. He drove a sequence of very battered cars. When one broke down he threw it away and bought another which was just as decrepit. Every franc he earned was from his writing. He never saved a single centime. He invested in nothing. He had no close friends. He never went home to his parents. He spent all his money in bars and on boys. He occasionally worked the streets himself, agreeing the price, doing exactly what he had been paid for, and then flinging the money back in the face of the man who had paid for sex. He provoked other people deliberately. He got into fights. He started fights. He knifed a friend once, but was let off. He was arrested for being drunk and violent. He spent four nights in prison. He swore at the presenter on television and then threatened one of the cameramen. He refused invitations to literary soirées at the Elysée. He had nothing whatever to do with women, but he never spoke against them. So far as I could judge he had never loved anybody. But, every summer, he went back to the Midi. He spent the days reading and writing, writing incessantly, draft after draft after draft. He had his books typed at an agency that took in doctoral theses, student dissertations and casual work. He then destroyed all his manuscripts. His prose was ironic, disengaged, detached. He watched the world as if it was a theatre in continuous performance, endlessly unfolding, act after act. He was afraid of nothing. He lived at risk.

I had never taken a single risk in my entire life. But now I was doing the most dangerous thing I had ever done. I was listening, and listening carefully, to Paul Michel. Beyond the writing, through the writing, and for the first time, I heard his voice. I was terribly afraid.

On Monday morning, dazed and slightly sunburnt, I presented myself for duty at the Archive. I felt reassured that, after all, nothing could happen to me in a university library. There was no security of any consequence on the door. The concierge gazed at me morosely, listened to my hesitant explanation and waved me away down a limitless green corridor with a mutter about "inscription des étrangers . . . gauche". The Archive was temporarily housed in three rooms buried in the remote outbuildings behind the classical symmetry of the university library facing the Panthéon. It had been freshly painted and smelt like a dentist's office, antiseptic creams and beige. The reading room had new, unmarked pine tables and green table lamps. I could see a young woman surrounded by boxes. Ink and biros were forbidden. The pencil sharpener was attached to the administrative secretary's desk. She looked at me with suspicious loathing.

"Oui?"

I began to apologise for my existence in hesitant French.

The secretary was of uncertain age and very aggressive, her evil countenance opaque with paint, every feature emphasised in lipstick, eyeliner and face pack, with orange shadows. I caught sight of the red talons ending her fingers, poised over the keyboard.

"Do you have a letter of introduction?" she snapped.

My supervisor had warned me. And in fact I had two: one in elegant, bookish French from my supervisor on Pembroke College notepaper. The other in English from the Modern Languages Faculty office explaining why I needed to use the Archive. The one from the Faculty office had more official stamps and was clearly more credible. But for one awful moment it looked as if both were going to be inadequate. She sat me down to wait, staring at fresh paint and blank walls while she checked out my credentials with her director. I passed the Archive consumer test within five minutes and was soon sitting beside an American, who looked like an advertising executive, peering into the microfiche. Finding my references was easy. Only one box in the catalogue was listed for Paul Michel. And there was only one piece of supplementary information.

Letters to Michel Foucault: philosopher 1926–1984
See FOUCAULT, M.

I filled in the slip and handed it back to the now expressionless painted face.

Immediately there was another obstacle.

"These letters are on reserve," she said. "I don't think you can see them."

"On reserve?"

"Yes. There's another scholar working on them. These letters are not available for consultation."

"Is he—or she—working on them now?"

"They are on reserve for publication," she hissed.

I suddenly turned obstinate.

"But I only want to read them."

"I'll have to check."

She disappeared again. I sat down in a rage. I had come all the way to Paris to read these letters. I glared at the innocent executive American, who had no obvious designs on either Foucault or Paul Michel. Eventually the secretary returned. She chanted a formula.

"The letters in question have been purchased for publication by Harvard University Press. All rights reserved. You may read the manuscripts, but photography, photocopying or reproduction of any passage therefrom is forbidden. You will be required to sign an undertaking to that effect. In addition you must make a detailed declaration concerning your reasons for wishing to read these manuscripts and the use you intend to make of the information contained therein. All publication, including précis, abstract or detailed commentary in any form whatsoever is forbidden. This declaration will be forwarded along with your name, status and institutional address to the holders of the copyright. This declaration will have legal force."

I nodded, astounded.

"Go into the reading room and choose a seat."

I sharpened my pencils very, very carefully while she stood over me, taking all the time in the world. Then I bowed with obnoxious politeness. I had turned love-fifteen into fifteen-all.

The box was large, brown, stapled at the corners. It was marked with the same title and reference numbers that I had seen on the microfiche. I opened the box, my fingers tingling.

Each letter was inside a sealed, transparent plastic sheath, but it was possible to open them and touch the writing itself. The earliest letters dated from May 1980 and the last one was written on 20 June 1984. They had been written at regular intervals of a month to six weeks. I peered at the handwriting—large, rapid and frequently illegible. Paul Michel had written on A4 sheets of typing paper which had rarely been folded. Some letters had no creases in the paper. There were no accompanying envelopes either. Someone had ordered the letters and each one had a number and a stamp signifying that it was in the care of the University of Paris VII Literary Archive, but that it belonged ultimately to the state. There was no typed index, no list of contents and no accompanying summaries. I had his writing before me, unmediated, raw, obscure. I shook my head carefully and tried to read.

I could understand nothing.

Each letter was carefully dated with the day, the year. Sometimes there was a Paris place name, St Germain, rue de la Roquette, rue de Poitou, Bastille, but rarely any number or precise address. I felt that I had begun listening to a private conversation and that I was hearing only one side of the encounter. At first it was all meaningless, an intimacy that retained all its secrets. The letters were all about the same length, four to six sides of A4. They were extraordi-

narily difficult to decipher. At first I could only make out
two or three words a line, then slowly, slowly Paul Michel
began to speak again. But this time he was not speaking to
me.

15 June 1980

Cher Maître,

Thank you for your generous comments about *Midi*. Yes, it
was a more personal book and therefore won't win any
prizes. Somewhere or other I am grateful for that. Those
whom our literary establishment wish to stifle they smother
with the Prix Goncourt. It was like a cushion over my face.
I have returned to my own chosen path. I was also surprised
and pleased that you noticed the episode with the boy on
the beach. I knew I was taking a risk. The public becomes
hysterical at the slightest hint of what could be read as
paedophilia. Their worst fears realised: all the French
beaches inhabited by predatory homosexuals bearing down
on little boys and corrupting their innocence. The
heterosexuals get away with it—think of Colette. But only
one review described the incident as disgusting. And as
for the Americans—well, that's what they expect from the
French. I haven't had to cut a word for the translation.
Perhaps I should have punished my narrator by murdering
him as Thomas Mann does with Aschenbach. Just to
bolster up their petty bourgeois morals. Did I tell you that
it was based on a real incident? I will recount the whole
story another time; it was unforgettable, bizarre. Nothing I
have written is autobiographical. Or at least not strictly
so, but of course every word is shot through with my
preoccupations, my concerns. Sometimes a figure, a face,
a voice, a landscape will make a shape in my mind, will
begin to inhabit my memory, demanding to be given a

new form in writing. That is how it was with the child on the beach.

I have never needed to search for a Muse. The Muse is usually a piece of narcissistic nonsense in female form. Or at least that's what most men's poetry reveals. I would rather a democratic version of the Muse, a comrade, a friend, a travelling companion, shoulder to shoulder, someone to share the cost of this long, painful journey. Thus the Muse functions as collaborator, sometimes as antagonist, the one who is like you, the other over against you. Am I being too idealistic?

For me the Muse is the other voice. Through the clamouring voices every writer is forced to endure there is always a final resolution into two voices; the passionate cry laden with the hopeless force of its own idealism—that is the voice of fire, air—and the other voice. This is the voice that is written down with the left hand—earth, water, realism, sense, practicality. So that there are always two voices, the safe voice and the dangerous one. The one that takes the risks and the one that counts the cost. The believer talking to the atheist, cynicism addressing love. But the writer and the Muse should be able to change places, speak in both voices so that the text shifts, melts, changes hands. The voices are not owned. They are indifferent to who speaks. They are the source of writing. And yes, of course the reader is the Muse.

I think that all I would keep of the common version of the Muse is the inevitability of distance and separation, which is the spark that fuels desire. The Muse must never be domestic. And can never be possessed. The Muse is dangerous, elusive, unaccountable. The writing then becomes the wager of a gambling man, the words flung down on one colour, win or lose, for the reader to take up. We are all gamblers. We write for our lives. If, in my life or in my writing, there was anyone who could be described as

my Muse, ironically enough, it would be you. But I suspect
you would rather be acknowledged as my master than as
my Muse. You are my reader, my beloved reader. I know
of no other person who has more absolute a power to
constrain me, or to set me free.

Bien à vous,
Paul Michel.

10 July 1981

Cher Maître,

You ask me what I am writing. Well, you would be the only
person in whom I would confide my work in progress. I
sometimes feel that my writing is the perverse and guilty
secret, the real secret, the taboo subject about which I
never speak until suddenly, behold, another book appears,
like a magician's trick. I make no secret of what I am, but
I hide what I write.

There were darker themes in *Midi*, darker than those in
The Summer House, which was, after all, simply the
anatomy of a family and through them, a perspective on
France. And France rather than Paris. You and I live in
Paris. I sometimes feel we know very little about France.
We only know what we can remember. I drew on your
memories as well as my own to make that book. You have
been too discreet to comment. Well, now I am working
with more dangerous, obscure material. The provisional title
is *L'Evadé*, and I wasted a morning worrying about my
American translators who seem to have such difficulty with
my titles and my tense systems. There are occasions when
I wish I spoke no English at all and therefore did not have
to quibble with their idiocies.

You take the matter of history, I take the raw substance
of feeling. Out of both we make shapes, and those shapes are

the monsters of the mind. We articulate our fears, like children in the dark, giving them names in order to tame them. And yes, *L'Evadé* is the story of a prisoner, a prisoner on the run, a guilty man who has not served his sentence, who seeks the freedom we all seek, whatever crimes we have committed. No one is ever innocent. I wanted to write a story of ambiguous liberation. To make the break does not mean that we ever necessarily escape.

And my methods? You asked about my methods. There are no secrets here. Like you, I read. I read continuously. I check my details, my dates, my facts. I do the spadework, the necessary research. But that is only the beginning, the preparation of the ground, the writing itself is work of another order. You will laugh when I tell you that the nearest comparison I can make is with the compulsory mass we were forced to hear every morning when I was being educated by the monks. Those frost-covered mornings, when leaving a warm bed, especially if it had been shared, was torture. Plodding in line round the cloisters, fumbling through our woollen gloves for the place in the psalms, kneeling in the gaunt, dark church, seeing our breath whiten the air. Sometimes, even here in these bare rooms, when I blow on my hands in the mornings, I remember those days. I can even remember the watchfulness of the monks when I glanced up to catch the eye of whichever one of the older boys I was trying to charm. The smell of old incense and white wax clinging to the choir stalls, the obscure and fumbling desire we felt for one another, and above that, the mass. Kyrie, gloria, credo, sanctus, benedictus, agnus dei. I had all the concentration of a fox in season when I was thirteen. The restlessness was brittle in my bones. Yet every day, as I sit down to write, the striped blanket across my shoulders, I sink back into that time. The mind floats with the shape of the mass, opening like a fan before me. I sink into the cold, empty space which it creates; I lean there on my left hand. I begin to write.

Out of memory and desire I make shapes. I reach back to those long freezing days in the classrooms, the gold above us in the autumn, biting our scarves as we ran along the edges of the paths, scattering the leaves. I touch the pleasure of sensation in that loss of innocence, the escape from banality into a vortex of desire and pain, our first loves, the first embrace of the forbidden tree and the joy of our escape from Eden. There is nothing so poignant or so treacherous as a boy's love.

Even then, I saw the darkness I see now. But it was like a shadow in the corner of my eye, a sudden movement as a lizard vanishes behind the shutters. But in the last years I have felt the darkness, gaining ground, widening like a stain across the day. And I have watched the darkness coming with complete serenity. The door stands always open, to let the darkness in. Out of this knowledge too, I will make my writing. And I have nothing to fear.

There is another shape too, which returns. One night, walking alone in the Midi, in a town I hardly knew, I was searching, yes, I suppose I was, looking for the men leaning against their cars in the dark, watching for the glow of cigarettes in the doorways, I passed the church. And I heard the scream of an owl rising in the dark. I looked up. He suddenly took off from the lime trees above me, floodlit from beneath, a great white owl, his belly bleached white in the darkness, his huge white wings outstretched, crying in the night, flinging himself away into the darkness. And as I followed his flight into the dark, the night appeared to be a solid substance, matter to be written. I cannot believe that I have anything to fear.

Bien à vous,
Paul Michel.

30 September 1981

Cher Maître,

How odd that your memory of the cold during mass should
be so similar. Our schooldays are a nightmare shared. My
most intense memories date from my childhood. I expect
that is a universal phenomenon. We lived in a large flat
in the rue Montgaillard in Toulouse. My mother used to
stretch the washing line across the street on a pulley system
attached to her neighbour's window. And they shared the
line. I remember her calling, Anne-Marie, Anne-Marie, out
of the window whenever she was ready to use the line. The
rents for those flats in the narrow street are colossal now.

I was an only child and spent most of the day helping
my mother, handing her clothes pegs, folding the sheets
and heating the flat iron on the stove. We had wood
delivered once a week and I carried the logs one by one up
the dark tiled staircase to the cupboard in the kitchen where
my mother kept her woodstore. She lived like a
countrywoman in the middle of the city. She kept tomato
plants and sweet peas on the balcony, their scent
dominated the stifling summer nights. I remember the sound
of dirty water, dishwater, washing water, being flung down
from the flats into the street, the shutters banging in the
night, families quarrelling behind locked doors.

My father was often away from home doing repair work
on the railways. He came back late in the evening, dirty
and tired, and was forbidden to kiss me until he had washed.
She was fanatically clean. She scrubbed everything; the
kitchen, the pots, the sheets, the stairs, father, me. I
remember the smell of that rough, unscented soap, when
my father opened his arms, scoured until the skin was red
and the hairs still damp, and called—alors viens, petit
mec. And I remember how I flinched when he kissed me.

My father was alien territory, to be traversed with caution,

but I knew every scent and curve of my mother's body. During
the hot days if we were still staying in the city, she slept
in the afternoons and I slept beside her, curled against the
shiny texture and white lace bodice of her slip. She smelt
of lavender and nail polish. I used to gaze, fascinated, at
the strange convex curves of her painted toenails as if they
were the single sign of a pair of invisible shoes. Sometimes
she slept on her back with her arms folded, like a dead
crusader. I crouched against her, feeling like an aborted
foetus, not daring to indicate that I still lived. When I did
my homework she would be cooking, leaning over my
books, correcting my verbs, my maps, my dates, my maths
while she pulverised vegetables, plaited pastry or watched
the sauce rise with terrible concentration. She bargained in
markets, dressed up to visit her neighbours, posed as a
glamorous and daring woman when she smoked cigarettes.
She adored the cinema. My father earned good money, so
they often went out. I was deposited with Anne-Marie, who
would give me striped boiled sweets and tell me terrifying
stories.

My mother came from the vineyards of Gaillac. Her
father owned his vines. They lived simply, but they were
not poor people. When the war in Algeria was over her
father was among the first to accept the pieds-noirs who
went to live there and who brought their knowledge from
the lost vineyards in Africa. Gaillac was known for white
wines. It was the arrival of these incomers that transformed
the wine production in the area. We went out to stay on
the hot soft slopes during the summer months. I
remember the house with its narrow brickwork and perfect
row of lozenge windows under the receding dogtooth of the
corniche, beneath the gutterless eaves which dripped on
to the gravel in regular fluted torrents during the
thunderstorms.

My grandmother talked all the time in a soft undertone,

to her ducks, her cats, her chickens, her indifferent dogs, her husband and her grandson. She seemed to be whispering secret instructions which no one understood. The villagers called her "la pauvre vieille" and said that she had always been that way, since the early years of her marriage. And they said that she had been beautiful, proud, and had liked her own way, but that when she had married Jean-Baptiste Michel she had made her bargain and slammed the door shut on her own happiness. He was a man who did not know the meaning of compromise or forgiveness.

There was a night when she ran all the way back to her parents' house, blood covering the front of her blouse, without her coat, terrified and screaming. Jean-Baptiste Michel came to fetch her in the morning, and she went back without protest, abject and defeated. After that she began murmuring to her animals. No one provoked Jean-Baptiste Michel without suffering the consequences.

The only person who was capable of stopping him was my mother. She was his only child. In her own way I suppose that she loved him. She stood between him and my whispering grandmother. I see her head raised from her vegetables in warning at the sound of his step. I see her wringing his shirts into coils, plucked from the aluminium tub, with concentrated care. I see her watching him at mealtimes, anticipating his demands. I see her reaching for her purse to give him money as he leaves the house. She always fed me before he came home so that I did not irritate him or dribble and jabber at the table. And sometimes he watches her carefully and she meets his glance as if there is an understanding between them. I hear her voice, low and rhythmic as a drum, reading aloud in the evenings. His broad back bends to hear her, his face is in shadow. He is huge, monstrous. I am watching Ariadne and the Minotaur.

She began to suffer from tiredness, a lassitude that sapped

her energy in the mornings. I saw the rings beneath her eyes darkening and deepening. She no longer went out to Gaillac at the weekends. Anne-Marie came to help her get me off to school and to give her a hand with the housework. Jean-Baptiste Michel refused to hear anyone suggest that she was ill.

"She's lazy, that's all," he snapped. "She thinks that she's too fine to work."

But even I noticed the whispering and silences surrounding her exhaustion, the terrible yellowing crackle of her shrivelling skin. She aged and shrank before my frightened glance. Her full breasts ebbed and her buttocks sagged. It was a spell working from within.

I came home from school. The bedroom door was shut fast. My father was slumped weeping across the table. Anne-Marie, her face set and ruthless, her hands clasped, stood before me.

"Your mother has left us at last, mon petit. She is rejoicing in heaven with Our Lady and the angels." She spoke every word with measured and devastating certainty.

I won a scholarship to the Benedictine school attached to the monastery and my father sent me away to board during the terms. In the holidays I was handed over to my grandparents in Gaillac. I never went home again. And I took my grandfather's name.

Bien à vous,
Paul Michel

Paris, 1 June 1984

Cher Maître,

No, I very seldom draw upon my own memories directly. But it is my past which provides the fixed limits of my imagination. Our childhoods, our several histories, lived in

the bone, are not the straitjackets we think they are. I
rework the intensity of that capacity to perceive, the shifts
in scale, colour; the silences around the table as a family
lays down their forks, the howl of a dog chained to the
woodpile as the sleet forms in a winter sky, the years when
the autumn never comes, but the winter grey, the mass of
wet leaves, coats the gravel long before Toussaint. I still
see the chrysanthemums, huge white blooms, gleaming on
my mother's grave in the pathetic cemetery above our
village among the vineyard slopes. I used to carry my own
pot of barely opening lilac buds to lay on the green gravel
of her grave. "Buy the pot which has the flowers still in
bud," ordered my grandfather. He grudged her even the
colours achieved. But up there in the empty, walled
graveyard, the flowers will open, in a gesture of consent,
when there is no one to see.

You asked about the men in my family, my father, my
grandfather, my cousins. I must be cynical—and honest.
They were what I have become—moody, taciturn, violent.
Mealtimes were mostly a silent affair, interrupted only by
demands for more bread. My grandfather was brutally good-
looking, a huge barrel-chested man with his mind adjusted
firmly in the direction of profit. He knew how to delegate
responsibility, but he trusted no one. He had his fingers
on every root in the vineyard. He understood his accounts.
He bargained with the wholesalers. He bullied the
inspectors. He quarrelled with the neighbours. He sent away
to another region for his barrels, where he got a better
deal. He made the tonneliers pay the transportation costs.
He was one of the first in Gaillac to invest in the modern
mechanical systems. He spent two years in Algeria and
came back convinced that France should abandon the
territory, despite its wealth and beauty, simply on the
grounds that we had no business to occupy another man's
land.

I see him walking the length of his vines, his old blue
jacket stretched across his huge back, bending over the
twisted stakes, the clippers in his reddened hands, touching
the mute, rough bark, his boots heavy with earth. Everyone
in the house was afraid of him.

One of his dogs bit a child in the face. I was ten years
old. I see the child, white, weeping, two deep purple marks
on the side of her nose, her upper lip, pierced, with the
dark blood bubbling into her mouth. My grandfather did
not shoot the animal as he could easily have done. His
loaded gun stood against the door of the lavoir. He beat
the dog to death with a cudgel in the chicken yard. We
heard a terrible sequence of howls and thuds. My
grandmother closed the window. When he came in, his
hands covered in blood, the child's blood, the dog's matted
fur, I said that the child, a neighbour's child, had been
responsible. She had teased the dog. With one stride he was
beside me and had seized my hair. Before my grandmother
could intervene he had broken my nose.

"That's right. Go and whimper in your grandmother's
skirts," he shouted, flinging me out of the kitchen.

The doctor, setting my nose in a plaster cast and covering
me with bandages, so that I looked like Phantomas, or the
invisible man, said, "Why did you provoke him, petit? No
one provokes Jean-Baptiste Michel and gets away with it.
Learn that lesson now."

When he was older, slower, he bought a television and
would sit frozen, hypnotised by the moving screen. When
he was dying he lay staring into space, with unsteady,
flickering eyes, as if he was still following the shifting black
and white images.

But I remember my grandfather outside, always outside,
his great arms browned with heat and dust, his eyes steady
on the wine vats, attaching the cylinders filled with the
poison he used to treat the vines on to his tractor, testing

the sprays. He employed two men, both of whom loved him unconditionally. He ignored my whispering grandmother. She spoke to him continually in a low, persuasive hum. He neither listened nor replied. I hear him leaving the house in the murky dawn, his feet heavy on the tiles in the corridor, the rustle of the dog's chains in the dust as he passed through the gate. Then, and only then, would I settle into my bed, secure, relieved, reassured that the house was empty of his presence.

I only saw him strike a woman once. I cannot know whether this is something I have imagined because it is a scene I needed to remember, or whether I really witnessed the event.

It is late autumn and the lights are on in the house. My grandmother is in the church hearing the catechism class. I have helped her today by cleaning the family graves. There is moss under my fingernails and my hands are chapped and red. I am outside the house, coming home. I hear raised voices in the spare bedroom which I share with my mother. The front door is ajar. There is mud on the doorstep and across the flagstones. I hear my mother's voice, deep in her throat, no, no, no, no, no. Our bedroom door is open and my grandfather, in his outdoor coat and boots, is standing over her. Her arms are rigid, her hands crisping the bedspread. She cries, again and again, no, no, no, no, no. With one muddy boot he slams the door shut behind him and I hear the flat smack of his hand against her unresisting cheek as he pushes her down. Then the pitch of her cry is horribly changed. And I stumble backwards through the kitchen, down the path, leaving the forbidden gate open behind me, out into the darkening vineyards, high above the village, gasping for clean, unheated air.

No one provokes Jean-Baptiste Michel and gets away

with it. Why did I so easily comprehend that lesson of
fear which my mother had never been able to learn?

You ask me what I fear most. Not my own death, certainly
not that. For me, my death will simply be the door closing
softly on the sounds that trouble, obsess and persecute my
sleep. I never court death, as you do. You see death as
your dancing partner, the other with his arms around you.
Your death is the other you wait for, seek out, whose
violence is the resolution of your desire. But I will not learn
my death from you. You revel in a facile dream of darkness
and blood. It is a romantic flirtation with violence, the
well-brought-up doctor's son dabbling in the sewers, before
going home to turn it all into a Baroque polemic which
will make him famous. I choose the sun, light, life. And
yes, of course we both live on the edge. You taught me to
inhabit extremity. You taught me that the frontiers of
living, thinking, were the only markets where knowledge
could be bought, at a high price. You taught me to stand
at the edge of the crowd gathered around the gaming tables,
to see clearly, both the players and the wheel. Cher maître,
you accuse me of being without morals, scruples, inhibitions,
regrets. Who but my master could have taught me to be
so? I have learned my being from you.

You ask me what I fear most. Not the loss of my power
to write. Not that. Composers fear deafness, yet the
greatest of them heard his music with the drums of his
nerves, the beat in the blood. My writing is a craft, like
carpentry, coffin-building, making jewellery, constructing
walls. You cannot forget how it is done. You can easily see
when it is done well. You can adjust, remake, rebuild what
is fragile, slipshod, unstable. The critics praise my classical
style. I am part of a tradition. It is what I say which disturbs
them, and that too is rendered palatable by the undisturbed
elegance of classical French prose. You can say anything,
anything, if it is beautifully said. My books are like a well-

known and frequently visited château. All the corridors are completely straight and they lead from one room to another, the way out to the gardens or the courtyard clearly indicated. I write with the well-swept clarity of a ballroom floor. I write for fools. But within this limpid, exquisite lucidity, that is my signature—and which I lose hair, weight, sleep, blood, to achieve—there is a code, a hidden sequence of signs, a labyrinth, a staircase leading to the attics, and finally out on to the leads. You have followed me there. You are the reader for whom I write.

You ask me what I fear most. You know already or you would not ask. It is the loss of my reader, the man for whom I write. My greatest fear is that one day, unexpectedly, suddenly, I will lose you. We never see one another and we never speak directly, yet through the writing our intimacy is complete. My relationship with you is intense because it is addressed every day, through all my working hours. I sit down, wrapped in my blanket, my papers incoherent on the table before me. I clear a space to write, for you, to you, against you. You are the measure of my abilities. I reach for your exactitude, your ambition, your folly. You are the tide mark on the bridge, the level to reach. You are the face who always avoids my glance, the man who is just leaving the bar. I search for you through the spirals of all my sentences. I throw out whole pages of manuscript because I cannot find you in them. I search for you in small details, in the shapes of my verbs, the quality of my phrases. When I can write no more because I am too tired, my head aches, my left arm is cramped with tension, and I am left irresolute, I get up, go out, drink, cruise the streets. Sex is a brief gesture, I fling away my body with my money and my fear. It is the sharp sensation which fills the empty space before I can go in search of you again. I repent nothing but the frustration of being unable to reach you. You are the glove that I find on the floor, the

daily challenge I take up. You are the reader for whom I
write.

You have never asked me who I have loved most. You
know already and that is why you have never asked. I have
always loved you.

Paul Michel

It is rare that a writer's papers are completely without
interest, but rarer still, as any historian will tell you, that
they contain pure gold. I copied out these four letters,
illegally, exactly as they had been written, over days, sometimes a line, a phrase at a time. They had already been paid
for, bought and sold on the market in writers' lives. Yet I
believed that I was capable of reading them differently from
anyone else. Under the yellow glare of dimmed and shimmering lamps specially adjusted to sensitive paper, I traced
his words, in pencil marks so faint that they became a secret
code. For five days I sat in the Archive reading his letters
to Foucault, hiding the letter I was copying under another,
disguising my papers under notes. The archivist frequently
came to peer at what I was doing. I told her that I was
studying his tenses, counting the times he used the con-
ditional. She nodded, unsmiling. But I was a panhandler, a
prospector, sifting my gravel and finding in my unwashed
dust grain after grain of pure gold.

In the middle of the second week I stared at the clean,
virgin paper of his last letter to Foucault. It was probably
the last thing he had written before the darkness which he
had described as a stain eclipsed his day forever. He rarely
corrected himself on the page. Yet I knew that it was his
habit to write draft after draft. Then I realised the truth that
was staring me in the face and had been clear from the

beginning. These were love letters. And they were fair copies, the only copies. The drafts had been destroyed. Foucault had never seen these letters, written over ten years ago. They had never been sent. None of them. Ever. They had been released to the archives by Paul Michel's "tutel". And the publication rights had instantly been purchased by Harvard University Press in the interests of scholarship. Whoever had stamped and ordered the letters had not always done it accurately. In all probability I was the first person to read them.

I sat staring at the pages, stupid and shaking, my skin tingling. I did not know how to react. I could not understand what I had discovered. I was sure other people were staring at me. I was afraid that if I moved I would be sick. These letters were no simple exercise in writing. They came from the heart. They were private writing. Why had they never been sent? Had he simply imagined the replies? They deserved a reply. They demanded an answer. No one should write like that and remain unanswered. I knew that I could no longer hesitate. I staggered from the Archive, clutching my stolen goods.

Paris became more and more unreal. I hardly noticed the tourists, the shuttered shops, locked for the summer. I stumbled through the water rushing in the gutters. I could not sleep at night. I lived on black coffee, rigid with sugar, and cheap cigarettes. I woke up on the Friday of my second week in the Archive with my head ringing. I heard his words as if for the first time, although by now I knew them by heart. *You ask me what I fear most. You know already or you would not ask. It is the loss of my reader, the man for whom I write. My greatest fear is that one day, unexpectedly, suddenly, I will lose you.* I got out of bed and dressed rapidly. My jeans,

which I had washed two days before and hung up in the
window, were still damp. I put them on anyway.

I had already made the most crucial decision of my life. I
would reply to those letters. I had decided to find Paul
Michel. Instead of taking the Metro to the Archive as usual
I set out on foot for the fourteenth arrondissement and the
Hôpital Sainte-Anne.

The hospital was like a city within a city. There were
gardens, car parks, walkways, cafés, shops, a security barrier
and a mass of huge, ancient buildings with new wings pro-
jecting outwards in black glass and concrete. The porters
indicated the general reception, but I walked some distance
before finding the steps leading up to bland offices and
automatic doors. Hospitals are strange intermediary zones
where sickness and health become ambiguous, relative states.
There are people distraught, hysterical, others resigned and
staring, the caretakers in white coats and comfortable shoes,
utterly indifferent both to the bored and the desperate.
There are three distinct groups ambling through the corridors, each designated by their dress: frightened visitors in
outdoor clothes, the shuffling wounded in dressing gowns
and slippers, the masters with their technological systems
and washed faces. I waited in the queue at the office. Two
women peered into their computer screens, ignoring the
hesitant row of waiting applicants. A woman perched on a
black plastic bench rebuked her whingeing child. Another
carried an enormous bouquet of gladioli, like a peace
offering.

All of them knew what service they wanted, but not how
to find it. I had only a man's name and an article in a
homosexual magazine, written nine years ago. And now I
had his private coded writing, his messages to himself.

Hidden in my inside pocket, the copied sheets glittered against my chest.

"Je cherche un malade qui s'appelle Paul Michel."

"Quel service?" She didn't look up. Her fingers were already flying over the keys.

"I don't know."

She didn't look up.

"When was he admitted?"

"June 1984."

"What?" She stopped the whole process and turned round to look at me. Everyone in the queue behind me leaned forward, expectant.

"You must go to the Archives," she snapped.

"But I think that he's still here." I looked at her desperately. "He was brought in because he was mad."

She stared at me as if I too was unhinged. Her colleague had got up and come to the counter.

"You must go to the Psychiatric Service," she said, "and ask there. They may have a record of what was done with him. They have a separate entrance."

She drew a massively complicated map on the back of an admissions card. As I left the general reception area all the people there stared at my every movement, warily, fascinated. The mother pulled her child back on to her knees. It was my first experience of what it meant to be connected, in any way, to the fate of Paul Michel.

It took me nearly half an hour to find the psychiatric wing of the hospital. And here there were no steps, no wide doors, no pot plants, simply a narrow entrance into a blank wall. I had to ring from outside; the door was permanently locked. As I stepped into a kind of air lock I saw the red eye of a camera mounted high on the wall, taking me in. I came out into a small lobby with a glass office exactly the same as all the administrative boxes in every bank in France. It seemed incredible that I had not come to cash my traveller's cheques. The women there stared at me inquisitively, but did not speak. I started on the offensive.

"I've come to see Paul Michel."

But the name meant nothing to either of them. One of them tried to help.

"Michel? M-I-C-H-E-L? Is he one of our regular patients? Do you know which service?"

I was confused. There were different systems even within the psychiatric wing. She looked at me speculatively.

"Does he come to the clinic? Or is he in the geriatric ward? Has he been here long?"

The other woman rummaged in the files which were clearly not yet computerised.

"There is no one here called Paul Michel," she said definitively.

"Look. He was brought in because he was mad. And violent. Nearly ten years ago."

"Il y a dix ans!" They sang out an incredulous chorus.

"You've made a mistake."

"Are you sure it was this hospital?"

"Call Doctor Dubé. He might know."

"Ecoutez," I began to insist, "he was first admitted in June 1984. But I rang just over two weeks ago and the woman I spoke to knew who he was. He must still be here. Please ask one of the doctors," I begged them.

"Take a seat."

I sat on a hard chair. There was no carpet on the floor. The blank cream walls smelt of bleach. There were no windows and the long white striplights gleamed in the tepid air. I waited, listening to the telephone incessantly ringing for over twenty minutes. Then, like a genie appearing from the tiles, a young, white-coated doctor appeared at my elbow.

"Vous êtes anglais?" he asked, puzzled.

"Yes. I'm trying to find Paul Michel."

"L'écrivain?"

At last someone had heard of my lost writer. I nearly seized the doctor with excitement.

"Yes, yes. That's right. Is he here?"

"What is your relationship to Paul Michel?" the doctor asked, giving nothing away. Panic stricken and suddenly inspired I told the truth.

"Do you speak English?" Intuitively, I sensed that this would give me back my lost advantage. The doctor smiled.

"Yes. I do. A little."

"Well, I'm his reader. His English reader."

The doctor was completely mystified by this statement.

"His English reader? You work on his books?"

I saw my chance.

"Yes. I'm his reader. It's crucial that I see him. I can go no further with my work until I do see him. And even if he doesn't write any more I am still his reader. I can't relinquish my role."

This was obscuring the issue with verbiage, and it was clear that the doctor did not understand the word relinquish.

"Eh bien, alors. Je ne sais pas . . . But in any case he is not here. He was transferred last year to the service fermé at Sainte-Marie in Clermont-Ferrand after his last escape."

I caught my breath and froze.

"Escape?"

"Mais oui—vous savez—they often do try to escape. Even in pyjamas."

And the man whose writing I knew so well, whose scrawling hand was now indelible on my own hands, whose courage was never in question, came back to me with full force. He was still there, still present, unbroken.

"Sainte-Marie? Clermont?" I repeated his words.

"Yes. I shouldn't think you'd be able to see him." The doctor shook his head reflectively. But I would not now be defeated.

"Did you know him well?" I demanded.

The doctor shrugged. "You've never met him? Well, he's not the kind of patient with whom you ever make much progress. It's sad to say that. But it's true. Why don't you telephone the service at Clermont?"

I took the number and thanked him warmly, then carefully negotiated my exit back out through the sequence of locked doors. I felt the women's eyes, suspicious, incredulous, attached to my back.

Jubilant, I ran most of the way back to the student residence. I had taken the room for a month in the first instance and had a terrible argument with the woman in administration who would only reimburse me for a week. I had less money, but now I knew where I was going. I scribbled a postcard to my Germanist telling her that I had found out where he was and that I was going to find him. Then I packed everything I possessed, including all the damp clothes from the window sill and the poster, gave the pot plant to two unconvinced Americans, and caught the 5.30 train from the Gare de Lyon to Clermont-Ferrand. Paris sank behind me; the flat, cut fields of central France unfolded like a checkerboard. I had a terrible sense of urgency and fear. It was as if every second counted, as if I had only hours in which to find him, to tell him that his reader, his English reader, was still loyal, still listening, still here.

Looking back, I see now that I had become obsessed, gripped by a passion, a quest, that had not originated with me, but that had become my own. His handwriting, sharp, slanting, inevitable, had been the last knot in the noose. His letters had spoken to me with a terrible, unbending clarity, had made the most uncompromising demands upon me. I could never betray those demands and abandon him. No matter who he had become.

CLERMONT

I ARRIVED AT Clermont-Ferrand in the misty twilight. The station was full of displaced tourists, and one anguished, uniformed courier trying to conjure up a bus in the car park. I was one of the last off the train and the car park was discouragingly empty. Clermont is built with volcanic rock in a gulf beneath a chain of volcanoes. It is a black city, with a huge, black, Gothic cathedral. I wandered the streets with my rucksack looking for a one-star hotel. Everywhere was COMPLET. Finally a tired woman crouched behind a dried floral tribute in one of the pensions took pity on me. She was nursing a vicious poodle, which growled at my appearance.

"You're English? It's nearly ten-thirty. You won't find anywhere tonight. Not this late. Just a minute. I'll ring my sister. She sometimes takes tourists. But it's a long walk out to her house. She lives in the suburbs. Shall I give her a ring?"

I was by now used to the French voice of doom. Everywhere will always be shut, the person you want unavailable, on holiday or dead, the restaurant reserved for a private party, another film showing, or the book out of print. I sat philosophically on an overstuffed, stained sofa and waited. And as always, obstinacy and persistence were rewarded. Yes, her sister would take me. Was I clean? Yes, acceptably so. Her husband would pick me up on his way home. One

hundred and twenty francs, cash payable in advance, breakfast included, shower in the room, and if I wanted to stay
for a week she'd do a special deal. She liked English people.
She often took in the English. English and Dutch. But not
Germans. I sat in exhausted silence until nearly eleven
o'clock when a bulging, slouching man cruised through the
door, pausing only to spit tobacco in the dust.

I understood very little of whatever it was he said as his
accent was beyond me, but I managed to murmur appropriate
things about the beauty of the volcanoes and the grandeur
of the mountains. I also managed to explain that I wasn't
there to take part in the music festival or the sky-diving
formations competition. I managed to persuade him to
smoke one of my cigarettes.

"I'm looking for a writer who is in the Hôpital Sainte-
Marie."

"Sainte-Marie?" He was startled.

"Yes. Do you know where it is?"

"Everyone knows Sainte-Marie. C'est en pleine ville."

He looked at me doubtfully and pulled up in front of a
villa bursting with geraniums. Another tiny poodle growled
round my ankles as I heaved my rucksack past the door. In
the morning I found myself encased in polyester sheets inside
a tiny room throughout which every available surface was
covered with various species of glass, crystal or china
animals; a terrifying array of Bambis, Lassies and prancing
kittens. Creatures of all sizes and colours were amassed on
the shelves and dressing tables. Some of them turned out to
be barometers which translated into a livid blue if the weather was fine. I decided not to unpack my books. My socks
and underpants were beginning to smell musty with damp,
so I risked arranging them along the window sill, which was
the only flat surface not rampant with adorable little beasts.

Monsieur Louet had already gone to work when I got up, but Madame, a duplicate of her sister in every detail down to the poodle, so much so that I began to imagine I had hallucinated the hotel, was wild with curiosity about Sainte-Marie.

"Is it someone you know well?" she asked, pressing bread rolls and croissants upon me.

"No," I said, gratefully wolfing down every crumb, "we've never met."

She was very disappointed.

"He's locked up, is he?"

"I should think so."

"The service fermé? There is a service fermé at Clermont."

"I imagine that's where he is."

"Did he—" she hesitated, "attack anyone?"

"I'm afraid he did. Lots of people."

"Aren't you anxious?"

"Yes. A bit."

"Let me tell you how to get there. You'll have to take the bus." She was already desperate that I should set out and return, articulate with descriptions.

The hospital was a great walled block, with a mass of interior buildings, like a convent or a prison, in the centre of the city. I found out afterwards that it had been run by nuns and that they still controlled the council that governed the hospital. The narrow windows were opaque, either masked with frosted double glazing, or patterned grilles and bars. The rue St Jean-Baptiste Torrilhon was at the heart of a dense mesh of narrow inner-city streets. I hesitated at the corner of the Voie Ste Geneviève, unable to find the main entrance. This was in fact on the other side of the enclosure. I had missed it altogether. I went on down the road past the double-parked cars. The building turned inwards, its back hunched towards the street. At no point were the walls lower than thirty or forty feet. They were covered in graffiti, mostly obscenities.

Then I saw, above a narrow door, a huge slogan written in giant black letters, curving like an arc over the entrance.

J'AI LEVE LA TETE ET J'AI VU PERSONNE
(*I raised my head and I saw no one*)

Beneath the words was a small bronze plaque which said,

CMP Ste MARIE
Service Docteur Michel

and beside the plaque stood the door, tight as an arrow slit. Beneath the bronze someone had written a poem on the wall. It was as if every official statement carried its own commentary.

Qui es-tu point d'interrogation?
Je me pose souvent des questions.
Dans ton habit de gala
Tu ressembles à un magistrat.
Tu es le plus heureux des points
Car on te répond toi au moins.
(*Who are you, question mark?*
I often ask myself questions.
In your festive garb
You look like a judge.
You are the happiest of punctuation marks
At least you get answers.)

I understood the French, but not the sense, not entirely. Just to the right of the poem was a bell. Sonnette. I took a deep breath and pressed the innocent white square. A camera

.eye, red, gleaming, flickered and swivelled behind the thick glass door. Then the buzzer sounded and I was let into an air lock, exactly the same as the one in Sainte-Anne. Inside were the same cream walls, artificial lights, airless, window-less corridors, the same reinforced glass box, two different women, with the same suspicious expressions.

"Vous avez rendez-vous avec quelqu'un?" One of the women stood staring at me while the other glanced down at her appointments book.

"No. I'm English. I've come to see Paul Michel." This time there was an instantaneous reaction.

"Ah, lui." They looked at each other and the older of the two, who had her bi-focals on a velvet ribbon, turned her gaze upon me with a distinct flicker of exasperation and fury.

"What is your relationship with Paul Michel?" she asked briskly. I told the truth.

"I'm his reader. Come to find him." This time I used the French word, "lecteur", but with such professional certainty that she posed no further questions.

"Asseyez-vous. Fill in this visitor's card. Name. Address in Clermont. Vous avez une pièce d'identité? I'll call Dr Vaury."

I sat down on the bench opposite the glass box and set to work on my inevitable dossier. Then I noticed that some-one had painted more graffiti on the outside of the office. It was the same hand which had written the mighty slogan above the entrance. And this time it formed an aureole over the grey head of the woman in the administrative bunker.

JE T'AIME A LA FOLIE
(*I'm madly in love with you*)

The text had been vigorously washed and scrubbed, but the

letters were still there, clearly legible. The older woman saw, me reading the slogan and shrugged.

"That's Paul Michel for you. Vandal."

I felt a shiver go through me. He was here and the writing on the wall was written in his hand.

"May I smoke?" I asked politely. There were no ashtrays to be seen.

"No," she said.

I sat silent, intimidated, seething with excitement.

Then, without warning, a young woman who looked hardly older than myself was standing, white-coated, beside me. She restated the facts without comment.

"You've come to see Paul Michel."

I stood up. She did not shake hands.

"Please come with me."

I followed her down impeccable, silent, empty corridors, lit only by artificial overhead striplights, yellow, muted. There was no sound. The doors were all shut. The floor was expensive soft white lino and smelt strongly of bleach. There was one painting, a banal green landscape hung high up, out of easy reach. She opened a door marked Dr Pascale Vaury and indicated that I should enter before her.

Her office was terrifyingly clean, but had posters, a black leather couch shunted into a corner, a huge, barred, vault-shaped window looking out on to a geometrical courtyard with long avenues of neatly pruned limes and impeccable white gravel paths. Through the thick lace curtains I saw passing strangers, some in religious habit, upright, marching briskly, others shuffling and bent, as if they were tortured, badly trimmed trees. The sun did not enter her office, but stopped short on the window sill, so that, outside, there was a glaze of bright light, inside, it was sober, muted, austere. The office was completely soundproofed. I could hear nothing but her movements and mine. She sat down on the other side of the desk and offered to speak English.

"I don't often get a chance to practise," she said, "only at conferences. Are you more comfortable in English or in French?"

"Well . . . I study French," I admitted, "in fact I study Paul Michel."

"Ah," she said, as if I had explained everything, "you're a researcher."

"In a way."

"Excuse me, but you are very young to be doing a research."

"Not really."

"Do you know why Paul Michel is here?"

"Yes. He's said to be mad."

She shrugged and half smiled.

"We don't always use those terms here. Perhaps I should explain. Paul Michel was admitted as a patient under Article 64 of the Penal Code. He has been diagnosed as a paranoid schizophrenic. He was a case of H. O.—Hospitalisation d'Office—that is, he is legally restrained by an ordre préfectoral. He has been very violent in the past, dangerously so, when he was *en pleine crise*. But in fact he has not been physically aggressive towards anyone, not even himself, for quite some time."

"It's his writing, isn't it? On the walls." My fingertips were tingling. He was somewhere above me, near me.

Pascale Vaury laughed.

"Ah, yes, that's him. To tell you the truth we were rather pleased. He got out. He always does. It's one of his specialities, but instead of escaping this time, he painted all the walls. You should see the poems in the men's toilets."

"Do you know him well?"

"Know him? Yes, I suppose so. I'm his doctor here. I met him first when he was at Sainte-Anne in Paris about six years ago. He has changed a lot since then."

"May I see him?"

"Yes of course. But I must ask you not to stay for very long. You will be supervised. I think that's best. And I must warn you, he may not be very co-operative. He is used to us, and to the hospital, but he is often very difficult with strangers. Don't be disappointed. He's not the writer you are looking for. Or the person you may have read about. He's very ill. He is in terrible pain, all the time."

"Pain?" I had not thought of this. She looked me straight in the eye, arctic, accusing, and spoke in French.

"Yes. Pain. Madness is a greater form of suffering than any other kind of disease. Folie—it is the saddest word I know. No physical illness is like this. It is the most terrible thing that can ever happen to you. It destroys every aspect of your life. It destroys you completely."

"Why do you work with them then? If it's so terrible?" I suddenly asked, puzzled.

She relaxed again. And returned to English.

"It's very exhausting. Very tiring. There's a lot of pressure from the families. And a lot of pressure to keep them locked up. And society has a terrible fear of letting those that they call mad live among them. There's a far greater tolerance of alcoholic behaviour, which is often not very different. I've been working in the French psychiatric system for seven years. It's a long time. You get attacked, abused. But you do learn to see things differently."

She picked up a pencil and turned it over and over in her hands.

"You see things more coherently. You accept things. You are more open. More tolerant. If I have a more generous, open mind than I had when I was a medical student it is largely due to men like Paul Michel."

I was moved, curious, disconcerted. She rose and picked up the telephone.

"Hervé? Oui. Ecoute—I have a visitor here for Paul Michel. Is he up? He is. OK. Tell him he has a visitor from England. We'll be up in two minutes. Ring administration and security. I'll tell the office. Yes. He may need a bit of supervision. No. They've never met. He's a researcher. OK. See you in a minute."

She looked at me. I felt two spots of red appearing in my cheeks. I was terribly excited.

"Follow me. Don't stare. But then, you're English. The English don't stare at other people like we do. You have better manners." She smiled, suddenly looking like a young girl. Her hair rustled on her collar as I followed her ringing keys back up the corridor. She kept her hands on her keys. The sound was perpetual, a soft chiming of metal as the keys turned in her grasp. She spoke a few words to the women in the glass box, then turned left into the lift.

As we went up, up into the maze of silence she talked a little about the service, the new clinic, the children's wing. I realised that the hospital was enormous, that I was encircled by a small city, a city inhabited by the young, the middle-aged, the very old, a city of the mad. But what was uncanny was the fact that we saw no one. There were no doctors, no nurses, no patients in the corridors. The wing we entered was absolutely silent. I saw nothing but green corridors of locked doors. Dr Vaury got out her keys, and opened one green door, which she relocked from the inside behind me. A handwritten note was sellotaped to the next door before us.

ST JEAN

She unlocked this door carefully and looked around as we entered. Then she relocked the door. It was a large open space, sparsely furnished; a television muttered, high up on the wall. The windows were barred and blocked out with thick, opaque squares of reinforced glass. There was dirt on the floor, crumpled paper flung behind chairs, the smell was unmistakable, urine and excrement. Two men, with horribly distorted purple faces and vacant stares, shuffled endlessly in the space. They were white, thin, gaunt; one of them had an arm, twisted and stiff, held against his chest. They smelt unwashed, fusty and old.

Dr Vaury greeted both of them by name and shook hands as if they were rational, living beings. But she did not introduce me, she simply nodded and I followed her into an office that was also a kitchen. A woman working among her papers looked up.

"Pascale—bonjour . . ." They began discussing another patient.

I looked at the filing cabinets, the begonia. The office was human, warm; but the stench persisted. It was everywhere. I felt a great wave of nausea coming up from my stomach.

"Follow me, please." We went on, deeper and deeper, into the body of Leviathan. Two more doors, unlocked and relocked. And then we were in a corridor with separate bedrooms. The smell was unbearable, a sharp acrid gust of recent human piss. I glanced through one of the open doors; the room was in chaos, with clothes flung on the floor, against the radiator, a broken plastic pot still spinning on the floor, the walls were smeared with fresh excrement.

A large blond man in impeccable starched white stepped

out of the room and greeted us. He shook hands with me. He was cordial, cheerful, reassuring.

"So you've come to see Paul Michel? He doesn't have many visitors." He smiled warmly. "This is my service. I shouldn't think you've seen a unit like this before. Don't worry. I've told him you're coming. Would you like to wait in the day room at the end of the corridor?"

There was no door. I went into another sparse, dark space with a chattering television, fixed to the wall, well out of reach. There were four heavy rubber chairs with metal tube frames. There was a large games table, bar football, screwed to the floor. And nothing else. There were no magazines, no pictures, no carpets. The walls were a dull green gloss paint. The single window was masked and barred. The sunlight was obscured. The smell of faeces was overpowering.

"I'll tell him you're here," said the immaculate white nurse, with a huge, glowing smile. "He'll be right along. Dr Vaury and I are within earshot just up the corridor if you need us."

I leaned against the wall, shaking. There was no ashtray, no ventilation. I didn't ask for permission. I lit a cigarette. I didn't hear him come in. At first the room was empty. Then there was a man standing terribly close to me, too close, looking straight into my face. He was thin, pale, unshaven, his T-shirt hung limp and stained against his chest. His eyes were alight—savage, glittering.

"Comment tu t'appelles, toi? You're English, aren't you?" He changed languages, effortlessly, faultlessly. "What's your name?"

Never taking his eyes off my face, he took the cigarettes and lighter out of my hand, lit one for himself, then, still never looking down, took two cigarettes out of the packet and gave them back to me. He put the rest in the back pocket of his jeans. He turned my lighter over and over in his hands. Then, reluctantly, he gave it back.

"Ah-uh. I can't risk the lighter. They won't let me smoke unsupervised."

"Why not?" I was horribly afraid of this thin, unshaven ghost.

He laughed slightly.

"I set fire to the ward."

"Do you mean to?" I sounded stupid, even to myself.

"Don't be such a fool. Nobody commits arson by mistake."

"But you could die." This was the least of his concerns.

"Well, at least I'd take some of the other buggers with me. What did you say your name was? They did tell me. No, don't tell me. I'll probably never be able to remember your name."

We stood staring intently at each other. He was my height, two long lines drawn down either side of his mouth. But it was the same brow, the same lift of the chin, the same eyes. I would still have known who he was.

"I didn't know you spoke English."

"Of course I speak English. I learned it at school. Everybody does. I've even read Shakespeare. They tell me you're studying my writing. Why didn't you study Shakespeare? He was just as angry as I am. In his own majestic way. And just as queer."

"I studied French."

"Did you? Give me another cigarette." He snatched back one of the two I had left, lit it off his smouldering butt and ground the fag end on the floor under his heel.

"What did you say your name was?"

"I didn't."

"Well, don't tell me, petit. I never ask your names. When you fuck someone's arse you don't ask his name."

I recoiled slightly, startled. He grinned maliciously.

"Have you ever desired someone's death? So much so that you feel you could kill by just unleashing your desire?"

"No."

I bit my lip. He gazed at me, glittering.

"You look like a fool. What did you say your name was? Are you another researcher?"

"Yes."

"And have you come to describe me in your little doctoral dissertation on the link between madness and creativity?"

He let out a hideous cackle and his expression became utterly grotesque. I shrank a little. He leered towards me suddenly, thrusting his nose into my face. Sensing hesitation and fear he at once pressed home his advantage.

"So you're another scrounging, whingeing, lying voyeur. You aren't the first, you know. I've fucked dozens of you."

Instinctively, I fought back.

"I'm not writing about madness. You may be a nasty piece of work, but I don't think you're mad. And I'm doing a dissertation about your writing. Your bloody fiction." Suddenly I lost my temper and shouted. "I'm not even writing about you."

Instantly, Pascale Vaury and the nurse appeared in the doorway.

"Everything OK?" she asked.

Paul Michel spun round to stare at her contemptuously. Then he said, mocking her. "Oh yes, Dr Vaury. Of course, Dr Vaury. Everything's just fine. Absolutely fine. No problem. Ne t'inquiète pas. Tout va bien."

The nurse shrugged and they withdrew.

Paul Michel looked at me with vindictive respect. He had drawn blood at last.

"What did you say your name was?" he asked, all provocation, dragging at his cigarette.

"You know perfectly well," I snapped.

His whole face changed. The lines changed places, his eyes widened suddenly. He smiled.

"But I keep forgetting." He took my arm gently and pulled me towards one of the rubber-covered metallic chairs. "Come, sit down."

He grinned at me, and the smile was full of imploring good humour and simplicity. Disarmed, I laughed. We sat down, even closer together, our knees touching, and smoked in silence.

"How long have you been here?" I asked.

"In this unit? A year." He continued to gaze at me with terrible concentration. Suddenly, he reminded me of my Germanist. It was the same owlish, interrogating intensity. I was disconcerted.

"And they told me in Paris that you keep getting out. Though I can't see how."

He smiled again. The same wonderful, transforming smile.

"Voilà," he said. "It's a professional secret. You can imprison the imagination. You can drug it into oblivion. You can even drive it mad. But you cannot keep it locked up. How old did you say you were?"

"I didn't. But I'm twenty-two."

"You're too young to be writing a book about me. You're too young to be reading me. Why didn't your mother intervene?"

I laughed with him.

"Remember—I'm writing about your fiction, not you."

He smiled again.

"Then—what in God's name, mon petit, are you doing here?"

And then I sensed the change. It was as if he had sucked himself back from me into a huge retreating wave, all that was left was the rush of washed sand and pebbles. Suddenly I knew how dangerous he was.

"Give me another cigarette."

"You nicked the packet."

He never took his eyes off my face as he stood up to remove the packet from the back pocket of his jeans. He was alarmingly thin. We smoked another cigarette. Then he said, "Who are you?"

I hesitated. I said, "I'm your reader. Your English reader."

His whole body flared for a second, like a dormant fire, touched by the wind, then went out into utter darkness. He sat frozen. Then he said, clearly, slowly, and without any gesture of menace beyond the lowering of his voice, "Get out. Before I kill you."

Pascale Vaury appeared in the doorway. The smell of warm shit invaded the room.

"I think that's long enough for today," she said as if we were winding up an exhausting session of physiotherapy. I backed away from Paul Michel's glittering, terrible eyes. I was so shaken and frightened that I neither shook his hand nor said goodbye. Instead I stumbled away after Pascale Vaury, down all the locked corridors of the mind. Her white coat was the sign of Orpheus, retreating towards the light. But it was I who could not look back. The terrible acrid, foetid smells thinned, vanished, gave way to bleach and polish. The doctor talked to me calmly, over her shoulder. I caught a word or two, but understood nothing. We went down all the empty staircases, which were untrodden, void. I found myself standing again before the glass office. Less than an hour had passed. It was all over.

Pascale Vaury was shaking my hand.

"We have your address in Clermont? Will you be staying long?"

"I don't know."

"Well, ring me if you want to visit him again. I can best judge whether it will be possible or not. Goodbye."

I was in the street, sick, nauseous, terrified and without any cigarettes. I looked up at Paul Michel's enigmatic message.

J'AI LEVE LA TETE ET J'AI VU PERSONNE

I turned on the blank cream wall, furious, and shouted.

"You say you looked up and saw no one. That's not true. You saw me. I was here. I've come to find you. You saw me."

A car passed. The driver stared. I was standing in front of the largest psychiatric hospital in central France, crying and shouting at the writing on a blank cream wall.

It was just after eleven o'clock in the morning. I turned away down the narrow streets, almost hysterical with disappointment, frustration and rage. I had found him at last, my lost writer, and he had turned me away, unwelcomed, unwanted, unheard. I had nothing left. I found myself in the Place de la Victoire, went straight into the café and bought myself another packet of cigarettes and a beer. I ate nothing. All afternoon I wandered the tourist-ridden streets of Clermont, hating the great, black, noisy city, the hawkers and the market people, the travelling funfair belting out music in the square. I haunted the cafés, washed my face in a public fountain, chatted with two drug pushers, picked at the bookstalls, chain-smoked drearily until my mouth tasted like an ashtray. It was nearly six o'clock when I climbed off the bus in Romagnat.

I was struggling to understand the keys my landlady had

given me when the door flew open. There she was, bristling with excitement, the growling poodle nestled in her arms.

"Quick! Quick! He's on the phone. Your madman's on the phone. He's already rung twice. He doesn't sound mad. Quick!"

I rushed into the hall, negotiating her mass of furniture, ornaments and lace tablecloths. I snatched up the phone.

"Bonsoir, petit. T'es rentré? Ecoute, je m'excuse. I'm sorry. I wasn't very helpful. I liked meeting you. Come back tomorrow. And bring me some more cigarettes."

It was his voice. I was overjoyed.

"Do you always threaten to bump off your visitors?"

He laughed; a warm, extraordinary laugh.

"Eh bien, oui, tu sais . . . pretty much. But not very seriously."

"You sounded serious enough to me."

"Be flattered, petit. There's not many people I take seriously."

"Do you really want to see me again?"

There was a pause. Then he said, "Yes. Very much. I don't get to meet many of my readers. Come back tomorrow. Promise?"

"I promise."

I put down the phone and kissed my astonished landlady. The poodle barked and barked, beside himself. We were on our second celebratory aperitif by the time her husband came home. I had told her all that had happened, every detail, several times, in a delirium of excitement and she was enthralled.

The next day was extraordinarily hot. It was Sunday. Madame Louet watered her geraniums at eight o'clock. By half-past nine the drops were already evaporating on the stones. There were no buses, but I proposed to walk down the hill into town. Madame Louet told me not to be silly, hijacked the car and off we drove, through all the empty streets, overhung by the great bells of the cathedral, to the narrow gate of Sainte-Marie.

I stood ruefully before the guardian dragon in the glass box. This time the corridor was not utterly empty. Two elderly women sat side by side on the bench, staring at my every move. The woman removed her glasses.

"Vous encore?" she snapped. I nodded.

"You didn't phone. Dr Vaury asked you to telephone if you wanted to come back."

"No. But Paul Michel phoned me."

"He's not a doctor. He's a patient. He can't just see anyone he likes, you know. You don't have any official permission."

"Can I speak to Dr Vaury now?" I began to panic.

"She's not on duty."

"But somebody must be."

The woman looked at me wrathfully. I was an inconvenient phenomenon. She picked up the telephone and quarrelled with someone on the other end. I walked up and down the corridor in desperation, my every step critically observed by the two fates. Their hands picked at their skirts.

"Sit down," commanded the woman in the glass box, enraged, slamming down the phone.

We all waited. My palms were sweaty with the fear that I would be prevented from seeing him. In the tepid, unmoving air and artificial light I sat gazing at my stained trainers, sinking into wretchedness. Then the miracle occurred. A hand tapped gently on my shoulder. I looked up and I saw Paul Michel, grinning wickedly, the immaculate white nurse standing behind him. I leaped up and for the first time my writer kissed me, three times, on one cheek after another.

"Bonjour, petit. You're a magician. We've got permission to walk round the garden."

His keeper smiled broadly. "He's on parole. But just in the garden, mind." The nurse vanished with a rattle of keys.

"Look. A clean shirt." Paul Michel straightened up. He was wearing well-ironed whites that smelled faintly of mothballs. He looked like a faded cricketing champion. His face was taut, ill, gaunt, excited. But there was the same, glittering, anarchic energy that I had found so bewitching, so disturbing. He inspected me critically.

"You'll have to dress better than that if you go out with me, boy." I stood there, grinning foolishly at him. He laughed out loud, a huge, mocking, ringing laugh.

"If you're going into the garden, go," roared the dragon.

"Calme-toi, mon amour," cooed Paul Michel, leering into the glass box. He sauntered away, while I, scuttling behind him, was left nodding apologetically to administration and the yellow, gaping faces of the fates.

Paul Michel knew exactly where he was going. We reached another narrow door with an answering machine fixed in the wall. He pressed the buzzer and leaned his face against the grille.

"Libera me, mon amour," he whispered, all charm and subversion. I realised that access to the garden was controlled by the office. Looking across the paved courtyard I could make out the dragon, peering from her window. The door hummed open and we came out into the sun.

Paul Michel stretched like a cat, closing his eyes, lifting his drawn, white face to the light. He took my arm and led me away down the avenues of limes. One of the nuns strode past, nodded to him, then stopped and stared at me aggressively.

"Who's your visitor, Paul Michel?" she demanded.

"My reader," he said calmly, "but I've got no idea what he's called."

"Behave," said the nun, smiling slightly, "and don't pretend to be madder than you already are."

"Yes sir," said Paul Michel in English.

The nun, who was tiny, reached up and ruffled his hair as if he was a child.

"Just you behave," she repeated, "and don't smoke yourself into hysterics." She strode off.

"That's Sister Mary-Margaret," he said by way of explanation, as we strolled underneath the lime trees. "She's great. I don't get any shit from her. She always says what she means. I like the nuns. They're more direct than the doctors. More open to new ideas, new methods. They're very tolerant too. Once, when I was in crisis and you know, smashed things up a bit, they put me on the strong drugs and in the locked room. She was the only one who could feed me, talk to me. I can't remember it all very well. But I remember her face, very close to me, saying the rosary, I think. Repeating the same prayer. I don't think that it was the prayer particularly, but the repetition calms you down. I got better very quickly after that."

"What triggered it off? Does it come in bouts?"

"Mmmm? Yes. I suppose it does. Let's sit down."

"You don't mind the nuns?" I remembered the strong anti-clerical streak in Paul Michel's writing.

"No, no," he said, ruminating. "Sister Mary-Margaret once said to me that most of the saints were considered to be mad. And that their opinions were often not very different from mine."

"Really?"

"Yes. If you think about it, it's true. The saints were always visionaries, marginals, exiles from their own societies,

Hallucinating Foucault

prophets if you like. They went about denouncing other people, dreaming of another world. As I did. They were often locked up and tortured. As I am."

His face darkened. I suddenly reached out and took hold of his hand. It was my first real step towards him. He looked at me and smiled.

"Am I a great disappointment to you, petit?"

"No," I spoke the truth, "you're not. I was devastated when I thought that you didn't want to know me. I was overjoyed when you phoned. How did you manage to arrange this?"

"I spoke to Vaury. She's all right. Most of the time. She's read my books. I persuaded her to let me out. I made armfuls of promises. She stood over me every time I phoned you. I don't have the right to use the phone."

"Why not?" I could not comprehend his world of bars and prohibitions.

"Eh bien, well, petit—to tell the truth, the last time I used the phone I called the fire brigade."

"You what?"

"Mmmm. They arrive with ladders and crowbars, smash the windows and let us all out."

I began laughing and laughing. No wonder the dragon hated Paul Michel. The man was without limits or restraint. He was beyond their control. They had no access to his mind, but he understood theirs perfectly. He was a free man.

"Mais, t'es fou," I laughed uncontrollably.

"Exactement," smiled Paul Michel.

We sat smoking silently together, for the first time, perfectly at ease.

"So, petit . . . tell me which one of my books you like best. I assume you've read them all if you're doing your research properly."

I nodded.

"Well, which one?" Suddenly he was like a child, demand-ing praise, approval. I hesitated.

"*La Fuite*, I think. That was the one which moved me most. But technically *La Maison d'Eté* is the best. So far. That's your chef d'oeuvre."

He said nothing, but was clearly very pleased. After a while he said reflectively, "Yes, you're right. *La Maison* is a perfect piece of writing. But it's cold, cold, cold. *La Fuite* reads like a first novel. It's not the first I wrote, but it has the emotional energy of a first novel. And of course, like every inexperienced idiot, I couldn't resist putting everything in. Everything I'd ever thought was significant, important. You write your first novel with the desperation of the damned. You're afraid that you'll never write anything else, ever again."

He looked ordinary, meditative, a writer in repose, the sunlight and shadow shifting across his face as the wind moved in the lime trees, and all around him the tall, bare cream walls of the madhouse, the high gates, the sealed windows. I think it was then that I made my decision. If I did nothing else for this man I admired so much I would help him escape from this prison.

We wandered among the geometrical arrangements of roses and box hedges, wonderfully clipped, as if we were in the gardens of a château. The wind was fresh and hot on our faces.

"How can you endure it? Upstairs? The smell, I mean?"

"Well petit, I don't notice it all so much. It was bad the day you were there. Marc was having a crisis. He had no idea who or where he was. Anyway," he looked at me wickedly, "I spent my early life having sex in lavatories so I find the smell of piss rather erotic."

I felt unadventurous, prim and middle class. He poked me in the ribs.

"You're so easily shocked, petit. And you try not to show it. Like all the English. I always wanted to fart at your literary parties."

I looked at him ruefully, and then felt that I was being teased.

"But you're just an exhibitionist. You'd fart and smash things just for the hell of it."

"True."

He sat down on the edge of the fountain and smoked another cigarette. I noticed that he couldn't walk for any great distance. He was terribly frail, insecure in his movements. Yet compared to the people I saw hobbling down the paths around us, he was astonishingly well-coordinated and powerful. I commented on the difference.

"Mmmm," he nodded. "I take fewer drugs and greater risks. I'd rather go on knowing and seeing the things I do— being mad they call it here, and they're not wrong—than become a sober acceptable vegetable. Most of the men in my unit feel the same. But it's a high price to keep paying, day after day."

A light spray from the fountain left glistening drops on the hair covering his arms.

"Try not to go mad, petit," he said softly.

"Could I help it?" I asked.

He laughed.

"No. Probably not. Some say that it's an inherited disease. Or a chemical reaction in the brain. The French treat it with strong drugs. But they also fumble about in your childhood for reasons. There are no reasons."

"What is it like?" I instantly regretted the question.

He raised his shoulders helplessly.

"Ah, well. What's it like? Do you really want to know?"

"Don't answer if you can't. Or if it would make you feel ill."

He laughed, his huge, warm laugh, and looked at me. Then I noticed the real difference between him and all the other patients whose faces I had avoided. It was in his eyes; his strange, glittering eyes were absolutely clear, unhesitating, still steady, ruthless, judging.

"No. Talking about it won't make me ill. Or send me into a terrible crisis. It's a state of fear, of real anguish, extreme terrors. At first I found myself running, rushing, as if I was being chased. You imagine yourself sought after, persecuted. Then you begin to live what you believe in. The most terrifying thing though is the way in which the colours change. I saw the whole world in violets, reds, greens. Nothing was subtle any more; just primary, violent colours. You can't eat. It is as if there is pain, pain everywhere. You lose track of time. Like entering a tunnel of colours . . . I put on an act. You know that. You're right. A born exhibitionist. But when I was mad I wasn't acting. I couldn't express myself, except through violence. I felt I had to defend myself. It was as if I was being constantly attacked. And I felt that I had no substance. I was transparent."

As Paul Michel talked, looking at me steadily, I held my breath.

"Just before I went mad for the first time I suffered from crises of anguish, a tormenting anxiety. I was unable to maintain any form of contact with other people. As I am talking to you now. Then I began to hallucinate. I saw tanks on the streets of Paris. Gradually I could no longer distinguish between the delusions and the reality. I was a stranger to myself. I was a stranger in the world."

He looked up into the trees. Then he said quietly, "You

cannot imagine the horror of dailiness. I found that I had been writing—on my knees, on my hands, on the inside of my right arm. When I saw the writing I knew I was mad."

He stood up and walked away from me, down one of the shaded paths. I stared at the changing patterns on the back of his white shirt as he moved under the trees. I left him alone. I waited.

Eventually he came back to me and stood looking down into my frightened face. He watched my fear for a moment. Then he reached out and cupped my chin in his left hand.

"Don't be afraid, petit. It's past."

"I know. You're not mad. You're not. Why don't you leave?"

I was almost in tears. He laughed, sat down beside me.

"Where would I go?"

"But aren't there—I don't know—day care centres, or something?"

"Oh yes, the Centre d'Accueil, and my God, the Hôpital de Jour. Where you can learn English and pottery. Ecoute, petit—I can talk English perfectly well and I don't give a fuck about pots."

We both laughed. Then I said fiercely, "I'll get you out. Come with me."

Paul Michel glimmered for a moment. The same flicker I had already seen which had filled me with terror. But it swept past.

"For the moment you'll have to come to me, petit," he said. "I must go and lock myself up again now. Will you come back tomorrow?"

"Every day," I said. "As long as it takes."

We looked at one another. I didn't explain. He understood.

Patricia Duncker

110

And so it began, a bizarre rhythm which took on a hallucinatory quality. Day after day, I flung open the shutters to
see the volcanoes of the Auvergne shimmering with heat,
the sky an aggressive, uncracking cobalt blue, becoming
white as the day turned. I drew my eyes away from the
silent, pustular domes to rest on the military ranks of china
creatures. Day after day, I took the bus down to Sainte-
Marie and spent all my time with Paul Michel. Sometimes
we talked without stopping for hour after hour, sometimes we
sat in silence and smoked. I bought him sandwiches, chewing
gum, cans of beer and Coca Cola, chocolate bars, cakes
from the patisserie round the corner, interminable packets
of cigarettes. All the grant money I had been given to study
his writing was spent on him. I made him walk in the
sunlight.

"You've got to get your strength back," I insisted.

Already I was planning the break.

And I retold Paul Michel every night, to the fascinated
audience of Monsieur and Madame Louet. She had gone out
and bought a book about schizophrenia and had discovered
that there were 500,000 diagnosed in France alone.

"It could happen to anyone at any time," she said, glower-
ing knowingly at her husband.

Pascale Vaury monitored my presence, watchful, but without interfering. I never went upstairs to the locked ward
again. I had permission to stay with him all day. We always
walked in the gardens. The dragon now firmly associated me
with Paul Michel's insolence and increasing energy. She paid
me the compliment of hating me too. When a week or so
had passed I brought her flowers purely for the pleasure of
witnessing her fury when she thanked me.

Sometimes we talked about writing.

"I make the same demands of people and fictional texts, petit—that they should be open-ended, carry within them the possibility of being and of changing whoever it is they encounter. Then it will work—the dynamic that there must always be—between the writer and the reader. Then you don't have to bother asking is it beautiful, is it hideous?"

"But that's not true of what you've written," I interrupted. "Think of what people say of you. They talk about your austerity, your classicism. You're nowhere to be found in your texts. There's just this cold, abstract, faceless voice. Even when you're talking about things that other people think are—well—shocking."

"And you don't find them shocking, petit?" He looked at me ironically, from an immense distance.

"No. Well, maybe a bit. But nothing like as shocking—now I know you—as that cold, cold perfection that you get in your writing—that absolute detachment."

"So I should be as I write, eh?"

"No, no." I was beside myself. I felt that we were touching the sand at the bottom of the river. "I don't mean that. It's just that if you think that fiction should be open-ended you'd have to produce rough surfaces, not these smooth perfect monuments you write. They're beautiful, beautiful. I love them. You know I do. I've spent years reading and re-reading them. But they're not open-ended. They're not. They're shut texts."

He looked down.

"And you feel the wind of cold. Is that it, petit?"

"Yes. Yes I do. That's not the problem, just a fact. There's a chill in that beauty, that cynicism, that detachment. A terrifying indifference. Ruthlessness, almost."

He looked at me intently. I felt that I had said too much.

Yet now that I knew him I could not believe that he had
written those books.

"I'm sorry. I don't want to sound critical. It's just that
you're the most passionate man I've ever met. And you're
nothing like what you write."

"Maybe," he said, throwing his cigarette away into the
sand, "maybe when you care, terribly, painfully, about the
shape of the world, and you desire nothing but absolute,
radical change, you protect yourself with abstraction, distance. Maybe the remoteness of my texts is the measure of
my personal involvement? Maybe that chill you describe is
a necessary illusion?"

We sat silent for a while, then walked round the fountain.
Once we talked about loneliness.

"It's one of your main themes," I said, sounding like the
judge who now had his prisoner locked firmly into a solid
dock of geraniums, "but you never talk about it directly.
Except in *L'Evadé* and that's the only book where you use
first person narrative. Ever."

I avoided pointing out that this was the last thing that
he had written, apart from the writing on the wall. He
looked down at the sand beneath his shoes.

"Are you asking me if I am a lonely man, petit? Or are
you asking me to tell you some more about my writing?"

I realised that the two, which I had always held in my
mind, distinct and apart, were now no longer separate. Paul
Michel and the hidden drama lived in his texts were utterly
and terribly fused. And this process was not of his making,
but mine. He was the end of my quest, my goal, my grail.
He had himself become the book. Now I was asking the
book to yield up all its secrets.

"I don't know," I said, hesitating. He realised at once that

I had taken refuge in the truth. We grinned at each other, all the awkwardness of the moment dissolving in complicity.

"You're an honest little bastard," he smiled.

"Well—there are two kinds of loneliness, aren't there? There's the loneliness of absolute solitude—the physical fact of living alone, working alone, as I have always done. This need not be painful. For many writers it's necessary. Others need a female staff of family servants to type their bloody books and keep their egos afloat. Being alone for most of the day means that you listen to different rhythms, which are not determined by other people. I think it's better so. But there is another kind of loneliness which is terrible to endure."

He paused.

"And that is the loneliness of seeing a different world from that of the people around you. Their lives remain remote from yours. You can see the gulf and they can't. You live among them. They walk on earth. You walk on glass. They reassure themselves with conformity, with carefully constructed resemblances. You are masked, aware of your absolute difference. That's why I always lived in the bars— les lieux de drague—simply to be among the others who were like me."

"But doesn't the—um—gay scene end up with people all trying to be like each other too?"

I had only been to a gay bar once. Mike and I had stumbled inside by mistake, thinking that it was an ordinary pub. Everyone stared at us. We appeared to be the only people not wearing white T-shirts and jeans. Mike panicked when he realised what had happened and the stares were becoming pointed and amused. We drank our beers with terrified rapidity and fled, avoiding a mass of fixed and interested glares.

Paul Michel smiled ironically.

"Tout à fait, petit. And they were always angry with me for embracing the hostility of difference. For insisting on perversity."

"But," I couldn't resist, "if it's so awful and difficult why not try to become a group? Be accepted?"

He glittered at me for a moment, then said, "I would rather be mad."

I gave up.

"I don't understand you."

We sat silent for a long time. I felt that I had touched the impenetrable hieroglyphic on the wall. Paul Michel would let me come no further into his secret world.

But there was something extraordinarily generous in him. I realised that he was incapable of being offended or of holding a grudge. Whenever I was put out, puzzled, locked away from him, he would immediately come towards me. When I prevaricated, he was direct. If I half spoke a thought he would finish my sentence. It was I who was sensitive, prickly, easily hurt. He knew things about me even when I had not explained myself. He always answered my real questions, the genuine demands, with uncanny intuition. He had a breadth of understanding, a tolerance behind his abrasiveness, which disarmed me completely. I began to understand what Jacques Martel had said: that in the recesses of his madness there was a grandeur, a simplicity of spirit that was incapable of lies, petty resentments or insignificant jealousies. He dealt in primary emotions, essential things. Paul Michel lived on the edge of his own sanity, day after day. It was this that made him so uncanny, and so dangerous. He would always be capable of killing me. Or himself.

Our days in the asylum gardens took on a sinister beauty. We sat in bright light and green shade, listening to the fountains, feet shuffling in the sand, and far away, the distant sounds of emergency sirens. Time became incalculable—and of no significance.

"You know, I'm glad we're always outdoors," I said. "I've never seen a photograph of you taken indoors."

He looked up at the height of the walls surrounding us.

"You're perceptive sometimes, petit, without knowing that you are. I suffer terribly from claustrophobia. And I seem to have spent my life behind bars and in tiny servants' rooms. When I dream it is of the oceans, the deserts, endless spaces. All the nightmares of my books take place within enclosed spaces. Even the *La Maison d'Eté*. All the family are there with the shutters closed against the heat, ready to cut each other's throats."

"Could we go out, then? For a day, I mean. Could you get permission?"

"Why don't you ask Pascale Vaury?" said Paul Michel, without looking up.

I couldn't tell if he really wanted to go out of the asylum or if he would merely come to please me. His tone indicated nothing but careful indifference. As I left the hospital that evening I made an appointment to see Dr Vaury.

Back in her cold clean room with the black couch lurking in the corner I suddenly felt too young, too irresponsible an amateur for this particular game. Her keys fell silent as she sat down. She was the mistress of the labyrinth and I was the servant of the Minotaur.

"You wanted to see me?" She gave nothing away.

"Yes. I wondered—that is—it's just that Paul Michel seems so much—well, not better—I wouldn't know—he's never seemed disturbed to me—or at least not really. I wondered if I could take him out for the day. I'd bring him back of course.

Pascale Vaury laughed out loud.

"Paul Michel isn't let out," she smiled at me. "He gets out."

I looked blank. I didn't understand.

"Listen," she said, "he has a disease which does steady, gets calmer over time. But there are dangers even when he seems reasonable enough. You've done wonders for him. I won't deny that. I wasn't at all convinced when you first came. I didn't think you'd stick it out. Neither did he. But you did. He's attached to you."

She picked up her pencil again and then her tone changed completely.

"I'm not at all convinced that what you are doing will be good for him in the end. If you hadn't asked to see me when you did I would have insisted on seeing you. You've been here all day every day for over two weeks. Most people are afraid of Paul Michel. Even some of the nurses are cautious when they deal with him. He can be very dangerous. Now he seems transformed. Oh yes, the humour, the energy is all there and gaining strength. But his aggression appears to have melted away. And it's that which I find sinister. We haven't altered his drugs. You've come here, courting him like a lover. What is going to happen to him when you go? Have you thought about that?"

I blushed uncontrollably at the implications of what she had said. I saw that my hands were shaking. But I held my ground.

"Would it have been better if I hadn't come? And he'd stayed here—violent, frustrated, locked up? Is that what you want for him?"

"The man is ill. He's not a prisoner. He is sick. And

answer my question. Have you considered what will happen when you go? What—after all this attention and devotion—his life will be like? You're not going to spend your life in a chambre d'hôte at Clermont-Ferrand."

All the questions that I had never asked rose before me. But by then I was no longer rational either. For years my life had already been dominated by Paul Michel. I was simply forcing my commitment towards the last point on the map. I went on the offensive.

"It's not your aim to keep your patients locked up forever. It can't be. If he's sick you want him cured. You've said I've made a difference. Even I can see the difference in him. How can he leave here if he has no one to support him? And nowhere to go? Let me take him out with me. For a day. Then a month maybe? On holiday. Anywhere. When did he last have a holiday? This is his chance. I'm his chance. Are you going to refuse him that chance?"

She gazed at me despairingly.

"I would need some kind of guarantee on your part, you realise that. He would have to be registered with the clinic or the Hôpital de Jour wherever you went. And with the police. There is a mass of paperwork involved to get him out. It could take a long time. I have to apply for his release through the Préfecture. He has to go before the medical advisory committee. And they must be in complete agreement. He cannot simply walk out of here. There are many things that must be done."

"Then do it." I was almost rude to her. "Do it. Let him go."

She bit back something that she was about to say. I pressed home my unexpected advantage.

"And let me take him out for the day. Tomorrow. We

won't leave Clermont. We'll just go out for a walk. And to eat. Do you need a letter from the Ministry for that?"

Pascale Vaury got up, unsmiling.

"All right. Go and see Paul Michel. I'm making no promises, so don't raise his hopes. I'll see what I can do."

I thanked her with arctic formality and fled away down the airless cream corridors, hunting for the right doors.

As I started for home that day I found that she had left a message for me in administration, which was handed over, very grudgingly, by the dragon. There were two terse lines, written in English on the hospital notepaper.

It will take 48 hours to get a day release order for Paul Michel. You can take him out on Saturday. I will tell him. Vaury.

I danced off down the rue St Jean-Baptiste Torrilhan. I was celebrating my first real victory.

As we stepped out of the asylum doors together, the women staring after us in disbelief, I took a deep, deep breath, as if I had been the one shut up. Paul Michel simply walked across the street and turned round, reflectively, to look up at the graffiti, written on the wall; the writer contemplating an unrevised first draft.

"Hmmm," he said, "no one's tried to remove my writing. Not quite balanced on either side of the door. But I was standing on two chairs and it was the middle of the night."

"When did you last come out?" I asked.

"A year ago. When I left Paris to come here. I painted the graffiti in March."

"Why didn't you try to escape then?"

He looked at me, amused. And said nothing.

"Come on, petit," he took my arm and we set off together, "let's get going."

Paul Michel looked at the urban world from which he had been so long excluded with a detachment that no longer even amounted to curiosity. It was the glance of a disinterested observer, the indifference of a man who was no longer sitting at the table, placing his stake, absorbed in the game. He stood smoking on the street corner, watching the young men, as if they were wild animals, imprisoned, behind a wall of glass. I was disappointed, even irritated by his attitude. He was neither grateful nor pleased to have walked free from his prison. What I had achieved was of no significance. The walls were within him. We drank a beer in a café. He didn't speak to me. Hurt, I decided to make a gesture asserting my independence. I went out and bought *The Guardian* and tried to catch up with the world of England for a while. He played the pin-ball machine. And there his absorption became complete. The flashing lights, electric bouncing noises and spinning mercury balls seemed to hypnotise him into absolute concentration. I glanced up from the foreign news to the sound of applause. A small group of boys had gathered around him. He was playing for enormous stakes and he had hit the jackpot. A flood of two and five franc pieces cascaded around his knees. He laughed, turned to the bar.

"Tu vois, petit. Je suis quand même gagneur. I still win. What would you like?"

I melted a little and drank some more beer. I noticed that he drank hardly anything. After a while I said, "You win. But you couldn't care less if you win or lose. Is there anything left that you do care about?"

It came out more sharply than I had intended. I could no longer deal with his utter indifference to the world and all that therein is. And although I could not understand my own motives then, I feared that his indifference unthinkingly included me. It could have been anyone who had come to find him. I was simply a pawn in some other larger game. I had not been chosen.

He did not answer me for a while. He simply looked out at the mass of people negotiating the traffic and the pavements in the summer sun. Then he said, "Come. I want to buy something for you."

We turned into the pedestrian precinct and he stopped in front of a boutique which sold, among other things, fabulously expensive hand-tailored leather jackets.

"Oh no," I objected at once, "I can't let you do that."

"How ungracious you English always are," said Paul Michel smiling, and pushed me into the shop.

I had been paying for everything so far and had assumed that he had no money apart from the coins that he had coaxed out of the machine. We spent an hour looking at ourselves in giant mirrors, wearing increasingly expensive creations.

"We both need a haircut," he pointed out. "We'll do that next."

I had never in my life taken any interest at all in what I wore. My mother used to buy all my clothes. When I left home and had my own money at college I bought whatever was neutral and fitted. The Germanist always wore jeans and heavy black Doc Martens with her laces tied three times round the ankle. She wore baggy white shirts in the summer. I had never seen her wearing a skirt and I don't think she had one. Paul Michel on the other hand thought that every detail in the presentation was crucially important. He noticed aspects of the jackets, shirts and trousers laid out around us that suggested standards as exacting as Yves St Laurent inspecting the summer collection.

"Have my clothes been getting up your nose?" I asked ruefully, reflecting on my transformation from frog to prince.

"No," he said. "I did comment the second time I saw you. But to tell you the truth I'd stopped noticing. However, as you are going out with me I want you to look magnificent. OK?"

The shop assistant was charmed rather than rendered desperate by Paul Michel's demands and criticisms. But the thunderbolt came when he produced a cheque book along with his carte d'identité and wrote out a cheque for more than 4000 francs. I was speechless. I was under the impression that he was penniless, had no legal existence and certainly wasn't in possession of a valid travel document and a cheque book.

"I didn't know you had any money," I said at last.

"I'm rather rich," he smiled ironically. "Didn't you tell me that I'm a set text, petit? There aren't any shops in the service fermé. I pay my keep at Sainte-Marie, you know. I'm not a burden on the state."

We stood in the street carrying plastic bags full of our old clothes. Paul Michel laughed at me out loud.

"Well, petit. And you lavished all that love and attention upon me with no thought of a return? No one can say that you're a fortune hunter."

He took the plastic bag out of my unresisting hand and flung it into a huge green municipal dustbin along with his own. The lid snapped shut.

"Now we'll go and get a haircut, drink an apéritif at the café in front of the cathedral and enjoy being looked at. Then we'll eat at the crêperie."

I put myself in his hands.

Quinze Treize was an ancient building in the cathedral precinct. There were many small rooms off the main restaurant space. It was dark and hot inside. All the doors and tiny lead-paned windows were open on to two small terraces beneath a squat tower containing a staircase. The entrance was almost invisible, under a low archway and past two huge nail-spattered doors. At seven-thirty it was already almost full. In the vaulted basement was another bar and a piano. We heard a woman singer warming up. I looked up the lopsided staircase and heard laughter from the top of the stairs. Paul Michel chatted to the man at the bar as if they were old friends and we were immediately swept off to an excellent table in the window. The waiter suppressed the little card saying "Réservé".

"Did you know him?" I asked, impressed.

"No," smiled Paul Michel.

"This table was reserved. Had you telephoned in advance?"

"No," he glittered for a second, "but I told him that we were from the Mairie and that I was one of the mayor's assistant secretaries, and that the mayor himself would be joining us later. That's why we've got a table for three."

I gaped.

"You what? You told him all that?"

"Mais bien sûr. Because if he finds out that we've escaped from Sainte-Marie the story will be perfectly explicable. If I am mad I probably do think that I work for someone important."

"You're impossible." I hid my face in the menu. I didn't want him to see that I was laughing.

I was also delighted by the way he had spoken of us both as escaped detainees. During the meal he drank one glass of wine, and then began to tell me stories. He talked then as if we were old friends; he told me stories about his childhood. He reflected on the meanings of madness. I listened enthralled. This is all that I can remember.

"Even in Toulouse the quartier felt like a village. There was a small community of Spanish, an even smaller band of Arabs. More live there now of course. This was in the 1950s. It was during the war in Algeria. One of them, an old grandfather, who always wore fresh white robes, sat on a bench in front of his house. He chanted the Koran, beautifully, the whole poetry of praise poured out of him, day after day. And the children gathered around him to listen. Until six o'clock struck. Then his whole discourse and manner were transformed and he ranted about nothing but sex and fucking; one long torrent of obscenities. The children would be rapidly dispersed when his granddaughter got home at seven o'clock and hauled him inside the house. But we would have had an hour of mispronounced French filth which made us rapturous with joy. They don't lock up their madmen. They give them fresh white robes and set them outside their doors to prophesy . . .

"And in our village in Gaillac there was a man with very long fingernails who would wander between the boulangerie and the bar, demanding ten francs from anybody who came past, and threatening to tear off your face if you wouldn't hand over the money.

"We're not all locked up, you know . . .

"I was an only child. I used to wander among the vines above our house at sunset. I used to talk to the scarecrows draped in scarves with lumpy stuffed trousers and old flat caps. My grandfather saw me dancing round a scarecrow, urging the creature to dance with me. And he shouted that if I imagined things I would end up like my grandmother, who lost her mind early on. She hummed and muttered continuously. In fact I am not like her. I am like him . . .

"All writers are, somewhere or other, mad. Not les grands fous, like Rimbaud, but mad, yes, mad. Because we do not believe in the stability of reality. We know that it can fragment, like a sheet of glass or a car's windscreen. But we also know that reality can be invented, reordered, constructed, remade. Writing is, in itself, an act of violence perpetrated against reality. Don't you think, petit? We do it, leave it written there, and slip away unseen . . .

"Do you know what they're trying to do to me in the asylum, petit? They're trying to make me responsible for my own madness. Now that's very serious. What an accusation . . .

"One of my hallucinations is that I am the last man and that in front of me there is nothing but a desert where everyone is probably dead . . .

"I tell stories. We all make up stories. I tell you stories that make you laugh. I love to watch you laughing. I shall never escape from this prison of endless stories . . .

"Would you like a crêpe sucré, with Grand Marnier and cream? Go on, I dare you to eat one . . .

"Have you read what Foucault wrote about Bedlam? Madness is theatre, a spectacle. We have very few words to designate what we mean by madness in French. You, the English, you have a galaxy of words for the demented: crazy, foolish, simple, idiotic, rabid, distracted, manic, absurd, insane. It is important to traverse all those meanings. Look at you, petit, only a madman would have come all the way to Clermont to find someone who had been incarcerated for nearly ten years, with so little hope of ever finding me. Without knowing who you would find."

He looked at me carefully.

"Madness and passion have always been interchangeable. Throughout the entire western literary tradition. Madness is an abundance of existence. Madness is a way of asking difficult questions. What did he mean, the powerless tyrant king? O Fool, I shall go mad.

"Maybe madness is the excess of possibility, petit. And writing is about reducing possibility to one idea, one book, one sentence, one word. Madness is a form of self-expression. It is the opposite of creativity. You cannot make anything that can be separated from yourself if you are mad. And yet, look at Rimbaud—and your wonderful Christopher Smart. But don't harbour any romantic ideas about what it means to be mad. My language was my protection, my guarantee against madness and when there was no one to listen my language vanished along with my reader."

I could not resist the moment. I took the risk.

"May I ask you about Foucault?"

His reply was as instantaneous as a bullet, savage, furious.

"No."

I could not call back my mistake. I snatched at words, mumbled my apologies. His whole aspect had changed; his face fractured with pain, then flared alight with cruel and extraordinary rage. He stood up.

"You disappoint me, petit. I was beginning to think that you might not be a fool."

What happened next took place so rapidly I never saw exactly what happened. A man appeared behind Paul Michel as he rose and jostled him slightly. The man made a comment. I didn't catch the words but it was leering, knowing, insinuating and unmistakably aggressive. The man nodded towards me, and his meaning, even without the words, was unambiguous.

Paul Michel hit him suddenly, twice, once in the stomach

and once in the face. He crashed backwards into the table behind us. The women leaped up, clutching their handbags and screaming. The whole room shuddered into chaos as someone seized Paul Michel by the collar of his shirt. I flung myself at the man who had laid hands on him and then felt my shoulders reeling into the pots of red geraniums, which lined the window sill. Two of them lurched on to a table outside, covering the food in damp earth and roots. By this time the man who had started the incident was on his feet again, and didn't much care whom he attacked as long as he settled the score. He went for me. I ducked out of range. Paul Michel smashed his head open with a bottle. There was blood all over the broken, empty, pottery plates. Everyone in the room seemed to be screaming.

And just as suddenly it was all over. A man with huge bare arms and an apron, who had clearly risen from the kitchen's steamy depths, dragged Paul Michel and his aggressor out into the corridor. I seized our jackets and rushed after him. Surprisingly, no one insisted on explanations. The management wanted us all outside the restaurant as quickly as possible. There was a woman pushing me, jabbering. I couldn't understand a word she said. Someone hustled her off to the toilets. All around us the clatter of Saturday night and the pounding music went straight on, as if there had been no interruption. I heard Paul Michel saying, with great aplomb, "I shall, of course, make my report to the Mayor himself . . ."

And the Director of Quinze Treize apologised profusely. I staggered after Paul Michel's rigidly dignified retreating back under the archway and out into the street.

"Did you pay, petit?" he asked, putting his arm around me.

"No."

"Good. Neither did I. You aren't hurt?"

"No. I don't think so."

He dusted me down and straightened my clothes. I had dirt from the flower pots on my new white shirt.

"That'll wash off. Soak it tonight. Come on. Let's go to a bar."

We walked away rapidly down the hill through the darkening streets. He still had his arm around me.

"Listen," I said, "I'm sorry . . ."

"Shhhh . . ." He stopped my mouth with his hand and pulled me round to face him. We looked at one another for one terrible second. Then he said, "I would never hit you."

He drew my face towards him and kissed me hard on the mouth in the public street, ignoring the people walking past us. We strode on down to the Place de la Victoire. Paul Michel was utterly calm and I was shaking with fear.

Three days later we were sitting smoking, side by side as usual, outside in the gardens. I was reading and Paul Michel was lying on his back, stretched out on a long stone seat, looking up into the shifting patches of light and shade in the lime trees, his eyes half closed. Neither of us heard Pascale Vaury approaching. She must have been standing there watching us for some time. I had no idea what was coming, but I think he did.

Paul Michel was so utterly unlike any other person, woman or man, that I had ever known. He had made no specific demands upon me, and yet he demanded everything I had; all my time, energy, effort, concentration. For something had significantly changed between us since the disastrous night out at Quinze Treize. The balance of power had shifted. I was no longer in control of the affair and the outcome was radically in doubt.

"I've got some news for you both," said Pascale Vaury, her face expressionless. I started slightly at her voice and looked up. Paul Michel neither reacted nor moved. He continued to gaze up into the trees. She addressed herself to his supine indifference.

"I applied for a temporary release order on your behalf at the Préfecture. I should say that I was under some pressure to apply. I have had a barrage of phone calls from your legal guardian. Given his prestige within the medical establishment I haven't had much choice. I have expressed my doubts. Nevertheless, the order has been accepted, subject to an additional report from the medical advisory committee. You'll go before the committee tomorrow. If all goes well you can leave on Saturday, Monday at the latest. I assume that you do want to go this time."

She paused, looking critically at Paul Michel. He sat up.

"I'll think about it," he said drily.

"You do that," she said, "and if you do want to go, behave better than you did last time in front of the committee."

I was terribly excited and anxious, crestfallen at Paul Michel's lack of enthusiasm. Pascale Vaury went on. "I've mentioned your successful excursion last Saturday." I held my breath. "It should count in your favour."

The fracas at Quinze Treize had gone undiscovered. The only mystery which remained, as Paul Michel gleefully pointed out to me, was an unsolicited letter of apology sent to the Mayor of Clermont by the management of Quinze Treize. This became a journalist's joke in the local paper towards the end of the week.

Paul Michel stood up, stretched, and yawned in her face.

"And where do you suggest that I go, Dr Vaury?"

She smiled ironically.

"Wherever you like within the frontiers. You can't leave

the country. But you have to decide before Saturday so that we can register you with the police and the local clinic— and fax them your papers."

"Well, as I say—I'll think about it." Paul Michel lay down again, arrogant and self-contained, dismissing her. Suddenly she leaned towards him and, with all the tenderness of a mother, she softly stroked his cheek.

"Ecoute-moi. Sois sage," she said, turned on her heel and marched away. I stared after her. Paul Michel lay looking up into the trees, laughing slightly. I realised, for the first time, that all his rudeness to her face was a form of theatre. There was an absolute trust and complicity between them. The hospital was his home. These were the only people he trusted, the only people he loved. I had nothing to say.

But it was as if Paul Michel was aware of what passed in my head. He knew I was jealous, disconcerted, insecure. He rolled over on his elbow and looked at me directly.

"It doesn't do to sound too enthusiastic, petit. That's why I wasn't. But I do want to go. And with you."

At one word from him my whole world was transformed from disappointment into joy. I was ashamed to be so dependent on someone else.

"What did you do to the medical advisory committee last time?" I asked suspiciously.

"I asked them to dance, insulted them when they wouldn't and then danced on my own."

"Oh, for God's sake. They'll lock you up forever."

"Yup," he sighed, "I felt like dancing and that's what they felt they ought to do."

He lit two cigarettes, gave me one and then said, "I really did have nowhere to go then, petit."

I realised at once what a terrible thing he had said.

"But your father's still alive . . ."

"He has Alzheimer's disease."

"Haven't you got any family?"

"And they'd like to look after a homosexual novelist who's abandoned his profession?" The scorn in his voice was perceptible.

I took a deep breath.

"You've got me."

"I know."

There was a pause between us.

"Can you drive, petit?" he asked casually, and the moment passed.

"Yes."

"Do you know anything about cars?"

"Not much. A bit."

"OK. I'll give you a cheque for twenty thousand francs. Go and buy a small car that works. That couple you live with will give you a hand. I'll make a few calls and tell you where to go. You'll have to arrange the registration at the Préfecture and the insurance yourself. Go to Mutuelle. They're the cheapest. I'll get Vaury to give you my carte d'identité to sign all the papers. You can register the lot in my name but put yourself on the insurance. I'm forbidden to drive. Only remember to give them your home address in Clermont. Say that you've lived there a year. And don't mention Sainte-Marie. You'll need your driving licence and your passport. You've got those? Good. You'll have to buy the car in cash. But I'll give you some blank cheques for the rest. Get a 2CV or a Renault 4 if you can find one. Tell me if you need more money. I'll think up a list of things to buy."

The expedition began to sound like a military campaign. My only doubt was the medical advisory committee. It was suddenly clear to me that he was anxious too.

"What if we do all this and then they won't let you go?"
I asked.

"It's no big deal. Three doctors come to see you. Vaury
will be there too. She must be pretty certain she can swing
it."

"Then do as she says and behave. You've spent so many
years acting as if you were mad . . ."

"And really being mad," Paul Michel interrupted grimly.

"Well, pretend to be sane."

"How do I present myself as sane, boy? What's sane
behaviour? You tell me."

"Say nothing."

"But I said nothing for a year. Nothing. Total silence and
they locked me up in the secure unit."

"A year? Oh God, that is mad."

He grinned like a wicked jester.

"Whose side are you on?"

I took hold of his shoulders and shook him.

"Yours, you bastard. Yours."

I smiled helplessly. He was anxious and afraid that it
wasn't going to work.

"Listen. Just answer their questions calmly. They want
to let you out. I've spoken to Dr Vaury. You're not HIV
positive . . ."

"Amazingly."

". . . and you haven't been violent for a long, long time."

"If you leave out last Saturday."

"You were provoked. So was I. Listen. You're not on drugs
you can't swallow. You get on well with me. We can get a
month at least. Maybe more. Maybe two months. Then I
suppose I'll have to bring you back for observation or a
check-up or something. But if you get through that they'll
let you out again."

"Will you stay with me when I see them?" he asked, his face set. My heart flinched with compassion.

"I can't. You know I can't. They won't let me. You've got to do it on your own. Be careful. Take your time."

We gazed at each other.

"For God's sake, Paul Michel. Don't, don't, don't provoke them."

He laughed. And I felt then that I had passed the walls and stood alongside Sister Mary-Margaret and Pascale Vaury. Our complicity was now complete.

And if this was an opera I would now be playing the introduction to the last act. I have replayed that summer, that year, so many times in my mind during all the summers since that it is now more than a memory. It has become a crossroads, a warning. My memory is a ghost town, still filled with heat and colour, dominated by the voice of Paul Michel. People often ask me to describe him. I tell them that he was as brutally good-looking as the old photographs suggest. He was uncannily still most of the time. He would sit smoking, fixed in one pose. People noticed him because he already looked like a photograph or a painting. He had dark grey eyes, astonishingly passionless, cold. And he used to gaze at the world like an alien on a research expedition. It was there to be observed, understood and then analysed. He was collecting data. But he was not playing, he sat outside the game. What I remember, even more intensely, was his voice, and his huge extraordinary laugh. Most of the photographs show an unsmiling man. It's true, he was like that; moody, magnificent, the king in an exile of his own choosing. But we became friends. And he used to talk to me; often when we sat side by side, in the car, in the bars, in the gardens, on the wall above the beach. We always sat side by side. So that I was most aware of his hands, his face in profile. But I will never forget the timbre of his voice and the way he used to talk to me.

I'll never know exactly what happened in front of the medical advisory committee. All I know is that afterwards he had a row with Pascale Vaury and she even raised her voice in the corridor. But they had decided to let him go. We had two months grace, from 9 August to 4 October, the week in which my term in Cambridge was due to begin. I spent two days in garages, banks and insurance offices. Monsieur and Madame Louet helped me with the paperwork. They let me use their telephone. They knew someone who knew someone who would get me a really good car, a bargain. They were anxious about the journey. I was setting forth towards no fixed address, and with Paul Michel. Madame Louet was convinced that he was unjustly imprisoned simply because he was charming to her on the telephone. She read one of his books, gripped from the very first page, and emerged two days later, scandalised and impressed. I became a figure from heroic romance in their imaginations. But they had a great deal of difficulty fitting Paul Michel into the role of persecuted maiden. Although Madame Louet said out loud what I had always thought, that if he was anything like the figure on the dust-jacket he was more than good-looking, he was beautiful.

I had last written to the Germanist from Paris. She had sent back brief one-siders telling me how her research was progressing. But something strange happened. She rang me up at the Louet's house. She was ringing from a coin box and so I never asked her how she had got hold of the number. We shouted at one another across a huge gulf. I found myself telling lies.

"I'm OK. Yes . . . I've met him. He's amazing. We have extraordinary conversations . . ."

But she didn't ask questions. She ran out of 50p pieces and the last thing I heard was this.

"Don't forget. I'm on your side. Take care. Remember what you are there to do. Remember . . ."

Then the electronic buzz cut off her voice. I was left shouting promises into empty air.

I had ceased to write home. I had not sent them my address in Clermont. The letters my parents sent to Paris must have been returned. I sent them a postcard on the last day, simply saying that I was going travelling with a friend and that I would ring them if we decided to stay somewhere for any length of time. Puzzled by her uncanny call, I bought a postcard to send to the Germanist. I stamped it. I wrote the address at Maid's Causeway. Then I did not know what else to say. So I left it inside one of my books, unsent, unwritten.

I waited for him outside the hospital door at ten o'clock on Monday morning. He came out on time, alert, boisterous.

"Well," he demanded, "and where are we going?"

"On holiday. Where else, you idiot? It's August. And anyway I thought you had to tell Dr Vaury where we were going. I left it to you to decide."

He let out a great shout.

"South. South. Let's go to the Midi. Which car's ours?"

He pounced on the 2CV and began rolling back the roof with the rapidity of an expert as I stowed his bags alongside mine in the boot. I looked at him carefully. He was clean-shaven, slightly sunburnt. He had put on weight. He was like a man who had escaped from the grave.

THE MIDI

WE DROVE SOUTH in a heat wave. I had bought various maps, but we didn't need them. Paul Michel simply told me which way to go. We drove down towards the A1 through the gorges of the Ardèche. There was a lot of holiday traffic and I had never driven on the right-hand side of the road before. And so we descended the green mountains, past pine forests shimmering with heat, past rough white rock, landslips, lay-bys with overflowing dustbins, rivers reduced to trickles, pursued by an infuriated tail of dangerous drivers longing to push the 2CV and its trembling novice into the ravine. Paul Michel didn't give a damn. He climbed on to the seat and screamed abuse through the sun-roof. He played rock tapes on his ghetto blaster. He even flung a Coke can at a frustrated Mercedes.

Then he said, "Pull in every so often and let them all go past, petit. Or we'll all develop heart conditions."

We bypassed Aubenas and suddenly swooped down off the mountains into the valley of the Rhône. We stopped in Montélimar for a drink. My T-shirt was soaking with heat, sweat and fright.

"Take it off," said Paul Michel. I hesitated. We were standing in a busy square full of little cafés. It was nearly 37°C in the shade. "Come on. Don't be shy."

I took off my T-shirt, very embarrassed. He stared at me

appraisingly, then washed out my already sodden white shirt in the fountain.

"If I was as charming as you are, petit," he said sweetly, "I wouldn't wear shirts. In fact I don't think I'd even bother to buy them."

I sat, soaking wet, much cooler, drinking espresso and smoking, under a plane tree. Paul Michel was relaxed, at home. He clearly loved travelling. I realised then that he had cut himself loose from every harbour. He had no house, no flat, no room. There was no empty space with all his possessions, cowering behind him, somewhere in the city. He had no addresses. He lived in the present tense. I began to wonder if he preferred it that way. We dozed in shady grass for most of the afternoon. When six o'clock passed we drove on south, always south. The little car was a symphony of rattles.

"Stay on the motorway and we'll drive through the night. There'll be less traffic," said Paul Michel, "and it'll be cooler."

He still hadn't told me where we were going.

We stopped at the motorway services south of Salon-de-Provence and he made a phone call. I watched the initial numbers 93.91 . . . he was ringing Nice.

"Alain? Oui, c'est moi . . . Oui, comme tu dis . . . Evadé encore une fois . . . Non, j'ai la permission . . . suis pas si fou que ça . . . Ecoute, j'arrive avec mon petit gars . . . T'as une chambre? D'accord . . . On verra . . . Vers minuit? Ou plus tard . . . ça te dérange pas? . . . Bien, je t'embrasse très fort . . . ciao."

"So," I said, as he pushed open the door of the glass inferno, "we're going to Nice."

"About 25 kilometres the other side of Nice, my little detective." He hugged me. "Come, let's have a shower."

"A shower?"

In fact the roads were so hot and so jammed that people had died in their cars. At all the service stations there were outdoor showers; a very fine, cold spray coming from concentrated jets on to a huge paved area. Some people danced into the spray wearing swimming costumes, some stark naked, some fully clothed. Paul Michel took off his watch and calmly packed his wallet and mine into the boot, pocketed the keys, took off his espadrilles and walked into the spray. It was eight o'clock in the evening. It was still 35°C. I hesitated on the brink, feeling the first fine drops covering my arms. Paul Michel joined a gaggle of shrieking, dancing Italians and invited one of the youngest girls, a lanky child of about fourteen, whose soaking black plaits were hanging down the back of her wet dress, to dance. The entire family clapped and shouted as they waltzed across the streaming stones, laughing and laughing.

When I close my eyes I see that image again. I see how much he had changed, how easily he made friends with other people, how every moment since his escape was turned into a festival, into dancing. He was not an easy man to know. He was difficult to judge. He was a mass of open plains and locked spaces. At first, day after day in the hospital gardens, I had come towards him, afraid of his moods, his sudden withdrawals, his potential violence. Now I saw him transformed. He no longer looked his age. He was present, close to me, aware of me every moment we were together. He gave me all his attention. Attention is a kind of passion. I was no longer possessed by my mission impossible; to rescue Paul Michel. I was no longer the one who was patient, waiting, giving. On that journey south he turned his face towards me.

Now they were dancing in a ring, now as a serpent,

drawing everyone present into the shower, two naked boys, a fat old woman wearing a headscarf, a man with his now streaming glasses still balanced on his nose. Paul Michel reached out and pulled me into that wonderful cold spray, and into the dance. Cars slowed down beside the burnt grass verge. People gathered to watch and the circle widened as we shouted, clapped and danced into the orange light, transforming the world into gold.

It was nearly two in the morning when we pulled up in front of the huge white gates of Studio Bear. It had been one of the most advanced recording studios in Europe. It was where Pink Floyd had recorded *The Wall*, although Alain Legras told me later that they had actually recorded the music in the concrete mushroom which contained the swimming pool's chlorinating unit, because the acoustic was better. Paul Michel said that he ought to install a plaque on the door and have guided tours. The studio was burned out during the great fires of 1986. Alain Legras and his wife, who owned a restaurant in Monaco, had bought the place and undertaken the colossal restoration, unending rebuilding, reroofing, retiling, repainting. The huge oblong spaces, galleries, corridors, remained unfinished.

I was so exhausted I could hardly speak. As the gates swung open I was flattened by a gigantic black sheepdog called Baloo who had slavering yellow fangs and was uncontrollably affectionate. Paul Michel poured a bottle of Badoit down my throat and put me to bed in a huge room with a balcony. I heard him closing the shutters, but I was already almost asleep.

When I awoke the air in the room was already tepid, a swirling warm wind touched the long transparent white curtains, but the shutters were still closed. Paul Michel must have slept beside me, for I saw his watch still on the table at the other side of the huge bed. But I was alone. I could hear voices a long way off. I rolled over taking both sheets with me and peered at the watch. It was midday. I felt as if I had been drugged. I got up and went in search of the shower.

The batteries in my razor had given up the ghost. I was standing stark naked surrounded by a sad pile of dirty laundry when Paul Michel came in without knocking. He looked like a freshly brushed panther, damp, sleek and gleaming. He took the razor out of my hands and kissed me lightly on the nose.

"Bonjour, petit. This one's dead. Use a plastic one out of my packet. Then come down and meet Alain and Marie-France. You probably don't even know where you are. Thank you for driving. You're a hero."

It was the first time he had ever thanked me for anything.

We were high up in the mountains just behind Nice. From the balcony I could see the valleys on the edge of the Alps folded into a sequence of barren precipices. If you looked closely there were traces of terracing all the way down the lower slopes. Houses hung in unlikely perpendicular places. There was a grey cement factory far away in the narrow crevasse at the bottom of the folds, overhung by a pall of dust. All sense of distance was curtailed by an opaque white glare which closed down around us. The pines already smelt pungent with the heat. I saw Baloo lolling on the terrace below with his legs stretched out across the tiles.

I didn't feel like the guest in a house where everybody else already knew each other, for it turned out that Paul Michel had never met Marie-France either. He had known Alain for over twenty-five years, but Alain had married her during Paul Michel's incarceration in the madhouse. I liked

the look of her. She was tall, stringy, forty something, but
casual and unpretentious. She wore no makeup and tied her
greying blonde hair up in an enormous scarf. She smoked
continuously and wandered around carrying things as if she
was not quite sure where to put them. They were obviously
rich people. The studio was now a gigantic unheatable space
with enormous fireplaces, vast cacti in pots, a baronial dining
table and eight-foot-square abstract paintings in lurid reds,
blues, greens, all primary colours, coating the walls. I guessed
at once that they were hers.

"You're a painter?" I asked.

"Yes," she said vaguely, "most of the time."

She had a son by a previous marriage who had just had
his car stolen. So there was a long sequence of phone calls
to him and to the police as we sat under the sunshades
wolfing coffee and brioche. Marie-France wandered about
carrying the phone and occasionally saying how delighted
she was to see us and how worried she was about the stolen
car.

"You mustn't leave anything of value in the Citroën if
you go into town," she said to me, "nothing. Not even a
bottle of suntan lotion. I don't know why it's got so bad.
Would you like a swim? I've checked the thermometer in
the pool. It's 27°C. You can take the matelas if you want.
I've pumped it up. Is pizza for lunch all right? Oh, but you've
just had breakfast . . ."

Even now, when I close my eyes I can see that terrace,
the industrial gleaming steel of her kitchen behind her, the
white heat just beyond the sharp line of shadow all along
the coloured tiles. I smell the pines. I see Paul Michel's bare
toes curled over the wall, touching the lavender bushes and
I hear Marie-France talking peacefully, about nothing in
particular. It was as if we had always lived there.

We shared the same bed every night. Paul Michel laid his cards on the table at once, without hesitation or embarrassment.

"Listen, petit. Sex isn't an issue between us. I don't usually sleep with my friends. Not usually. So don't be afraid of me. And come to bed."

Ever since his first kiss after the punch-up at Quinze Treize it had been an issue in my mind. I was relieved and disappointed. I let both emotions show. I sat down on the bed with my back to him, my elbows on my knees and stared gloomily at the hostile mosquitoes circling above the lamp.

"Don't I get to have an opinion?"

Paul Michel laughed uproariously.

"Tiens! I've never seen a clearer case of disappointed virginity. Come here."

I turned round, indignant. He held out his arms.

I was used to the smell of his body; warm grass, cigarettes, chlorine from the swimming pool, but not the weight or the strength in him. He had been so thin when I first saw him; brittle, skin flaking, white faced, unshaven, like a phantom. Now he was heavier, sunburnt, all his sexual power returning. He took hold of my shoulders, still laughing, and sent me sprawling across the bed on my back. Then he pinned me down with his whole body, pushing his right knee between my legs.

"Yield," said Paul Michel, shaking with laughter.

He pulled back a little, grinning, his face barely an inch from my own. Then he paused for a second, intent as a cat. He kissed me very carefully, very gently.

"You never have . . .?"

"Not since school. And then it wasn't like this . . ."

"Ah, masturbation in the showers?"

"A bit . . ." He undid my flies, pulling the buckle of my belt back so that it bit into my stomach.

"Got any scars? Any tattoos?" He was still grinning wickedly, like one of the goblin men offering poisoned fruit.

"Don't think so . . ." He cupped my balls in his right hand. My mind went blank.

"You'd remember a tattoo, petit." Paul Michel remained absolutely practical, utterly calm. "I'm not going to fuck you as I haven't got any condoms. Did the big boys bugger you senseless at school?"

I sank down into his arms, every nerve alert with terror.

"Not that I remember."

My voice came from a long way away, unrecognisable. I felt the breath of his laughter in my ear.

"You'd remember that too if they had, my love."

I had a terrible sensation of urgency. Paul Michel took his time. He talked to me quietly. I had no idea what he was saying. I ceased to understand anything except his hands upon my body. Then I lost all control of myself. I fell headlong down a tunnel that had no end. I heard Paul Michel's voice coming towards me down a chute.

"Steady, petit, steady, breathe."

I felt his hands on my back. I was on the edge of a precipice. I could still see the room, smell the hot night, feel his breathing against my face. Then everything vanished as I came against his bare stomach. He caught me with all the tenderness of a concrete breakwater. I arrived on the other side, dizzy, terrified and overjoyed.

When I looked into his face he was still laughing.

"There," he said, "we should have done that weeks ago. But Pascale Vaury would have had us both arrested."

We stripped off whatever we were still wearing and put out the light. He pulled the sheet up round my ears and asked me if I had plugged in the electric device for poisoning the mosquitoes. I felt aggrieved.

"How can you think of things like that?"

His laughter joined the warm night.

"OK. But don't blame me if your beauty is marred by a mass of itching red bites."

He held me in his arms, leaning all his weight against me. Then he said, "You deal with the mosquitoes and I'll buy some condoms. You're amazing, you English. You take a long time getting there, but when you do, you go all the way."

I was frightened that something would change between us. I was terrified of losing him. I held on to him that night as if I were drowning.

He took such pleasure in things that no one else would ever have noticed. As we walked up the endless stone steps to the bar in the square he suddenly leaned against a battered door and began laughing and laughing. I followed his glance and saw some music inscribed on glazed tiles beside a pink corridor.

It meant nothing to me whatsoever.

"Sing it, petit," he urged, hugging me.

I slowly read the music off the wall. DO—ME—SI— LA—DO—RE. It still made no sense.

"Domicile adoré, silly," he translated. "Perfect. Perfect kitsch. Being an SDF I enjoy other people's uninhibited domesticity."

"What's an SDF?"

"Sans domicile fixe," he laughed. "The homeless to you."

"As long as I have a home you have one," I snapped fiercely. I hated his assumption that he was outside every structure that ties all of us to life. He put his arm around me.

"I love you English. You're so unexpectedly romantic. Did you know that petit?"

"Don't patronise me," I retaliated.

"Good heavens. Aggressive with it," said Paul Michel amiably. "Have one of my cigarettes. It's such a pleasure not to be rationed any more."

As we climbed upwards, always upwards, in the cool of the day, we felt that we were being watched by women hidden behind the shutters, by a black cat with golden eyes, high in an alcove. Someone else had decorated their window with tasteless erotic statues of nymphs, only just failing to cover their genitals with parted fingers. In front of this three-dimensional pornography in orange stone was a torrent of trailing geraniums.

Paul Michel stopped to coil the red and green streamers round the women, hiding their breasts and thighs in foliage. I was appalled that he dared to interfere with other people's window-boxes.

"Come on. Don't . . . Please . . . we'll get arrested."

He strode after me taking the steps two at a time.

"I always cover up the women, petit. But I spend hours prising the fig leaves off Hercules."

"Remind me never to take you to a museum. You'd probably molest all the statues."

He laughed and took up a piece of charcoal that was oozing out under a cellar door. Before I could stop him he had written jubilantly across the wall.

VIVE MOI

I was too strongly in agreement with the sentiment expressed to object.

He always knew which way to go. I suppose that even if buildings, roads, shops, change their faces they are just the surface of things. Landscapes don't change. At the end of August the unnatural, uncanny heat began to increase. Many of the holidaymakers went home. Paul Michel took me to a beach on the east side of the city. It was almost hidden by the port. There were several tramps living on the steps above the port. They never asked for money. They seemed to be comfortably installed in a mass of rags and cardboard boxes which looked like a pantomime shelter. Paul Michel clambered past them, unhesitating. There were no signposts to indicate that the beach was there. You had to mount the breakwater, and only then could you see the steps, the narrow band of clean white sand and the great rocks below. Just above the beach, perched among the overhanging rocks, was a little café, bleached wooden boards balanced on huge tar barrels above the sea. The prices were affordable. It was the first time that I had bought a beer without having financial qualms throughout all the weeks we had been in the Midi, even though I had long since ceased to pay for anything substantial. We had an argument in the car. Paul Michel waved my objections aside.

"Listen petit, I haven't spent any money for nearly ten years. You're a poor student. I'm a rich prince. Why not lie back and let me write the cheques? I owe you for all those cakes and cigarettes that you brought to me in the hospital."

I gave in. In the end I always gave in.

It was the first week of September and the heat enclosed us in a huge humid bubble of warm air. We went to the beach every day and spent our time swimming, lying dozing on the sand or doing nothing in the café. I noticed that he didn't give a shit what other people thought. He would walk along the promenade with his arm around me, kiss me whenever he felt like doing so, spend time watching me intently as if he wanted to remember every muscle and every bone.

It was I who posed the first questions. We were sitting with our feet through the railings, looking out at the waves and the windsurfers scudding past at terrifying angles. I was very abrupt. I didn't know how to begin gently.

"What's going to happen at the end of the summer? I have to take you back. But they'll let you out again. I know they will. What should we do?"

Paul Michel looked at me for a moment. But he was wearing dark glasses so I couldn't see his eyes.

"That's a long way away, petit."

"It's three weeks."

"Like I say. A long way ahead."

"But it's not."

He shrugged. Then he said, "What do you want me to say? There is no future. You're trying to live something that doesn't exist."

"But we have to have some idea. Make some kind of plan," I insisted. He turned round to face me, but didn't take off his glasses. He took both my hands in his own.

"Sois raisonnable, mon amour. You have a doctorate to write. I wish to be transformed into a monument of scholarly authority and you've undertaken the task." He grinned again.

"So . . . you will take me back to the loving care of Pascale Vaury and her cohorts of sadists. You will then proceed to England, marching with military precision, and take up your studies again. You will write to me whenever your schedule allows, usually with academic queries on my texts. Is that clear?"

I lost my temper.

"No. It's not clear. There's no way that I'm letting you get locked up again in that inferno. We'll get you past the medical commission and then we'll go back to Paris. We'll find somewhere to live. I'll get a job or something. You have to start writing again."

He let out a wild cackle of laughter and dropped my hands.

"Ah . . . well, in that case . . ." He lit a cigarette. "My God, petit, you ought to be riding a white horse and bearing an ensign. You take your role of saviour much too seriously."

I got up and left him there in the café. I didn't want him to see that I was crying, with anger, frustration and pain. He left me alone on the beach for an hour or so. Then he came down and rubbed wet sand on to my back. I hadn't heard him approaching.

"Listen, petit," he said gently, "you are twenty-two and very much in love. I am forty-six and a certified lunatic. You are much more likely to be insane than I am."

I couldn't help it. I laughed.

"I'd rather be insane my way than yours," I said. He was still wearing his dark glasses. I couldn't see his eyes.

"You've got no respect," he said easily. "Come on. Let's go into the sea again before we go home."

That night as we ate supper on the terrace the heat thickened, like a hand across my mouth. Marie-France had listened to the weather forecast. We were expecting a storm.

In fact we saw it coming. A vast dark mass appeared in the valley beyond the city. The light became violet, lurid. It was as if we were suddenly placed on a stage, with the lights set for the final act. We could smell the damp menace of water in the humid air.

"Close all the windows—shutters too," cried Marie-France, picking up a random sequence of objects from the table. We rushed around Studio Bear, banging all the windows shut.

I had reached our room when the first roar of wind pulled the shutter out of my hand, hurling it back against the wall of the house with a crash. I saw Alain Legras struggling with the parasols out by the swimming pool. The air was charged, apocalyptic. I had just mastered the shutters when a great snap of thunder broke over us. The glasses on the bedside table tinkled against one another and all the lights went out. I was completely disoriented by the sudden advent of the storm and stood there stupidly, clutching the white lace of the swaying curtains. Paul Michel appeared in the doorway, holding his cigarette lighter out before him.

"Come downstairs, petit," he said gently. "We've got candles. Are you frightened of thunderstorms?"

"No. Not especially."

But I had never seen a storm like this one. We sat round three candles on the kitchen table amid a crescendo of thunderclaps. The lightning made every object around us suddenly luminous and sinister. Alain Legras took out a bottle of eau de vie to give us all courage. Then, terrifyingly close, a long serrated bolt of fork lightning cut the valley in half. We all tingled and cried out at the touch of its force, as thousands of volts entered the earth. And then came the rain.

Within seconds the terrace was awash, water poured out

of the gutters, gullies appeared in the garden, all the roots of Marie-France's iris plantations were revealed, naked and exposed as the earth washed past in a torrent of mud. We saw branches wrenched from the trees, heard something falling into the swimming pool. Baloo, lying by the doorway, raised his head and began howling. We worried about the cars, parked in a lay-by under a walnut tree opposite the gates. Alain unplugged the television and the video just in case the lightning touched the house. Paul Michel sat smoking calmly, holding my hand. He watched the world as he watched the storm, observant, indifferent; the cold gaze which I now feared.

It was more than an hour before the storm passed on, moving inland, leaving us without electric light in the dripping dark. Alain and I put on anoraks and wellingtons and went down to the road to see what had happened to the cars. There were many branches scattered on the steps and water swirled in and round the potholes in the roadway. The cars were still there, apparently undamaged. We had left one window of the Citroën open and the seats were soaking. There was a pond of water on the floor. Later, we heard that three people had been killed at a campsite near Cagnes-sur-Mer and that several caravans had been washed away. More serious damage occurred at a village in the Var where one of the bridges was swept away by the flash flood and all the houses in the main street had been invaded by mud. The older Roman bridge with its elegant curving arch and narrow brickwork had held, and was still there straddling the river's brown, rushing mass. Nearly eight people were known to be dead and many more who had been on holiday at the local camping site were unaccounted for. There were harrowing pictures of destruction on the television. The area was declared a disaster area. We had got off lightly.

But the effect of the storm was to transform the season.
It was now inescapably September. We still went to the
beach, but we came home early in the evenings. And something had changed again between us. Paul Michel now began
to talk to me in a way that he had never done before. It
was as if he had made a decision. He would no longer hide
behind his mask of cynicism. We sat side by side in the
beach café looking out to sea. It was the twenty-sixth of
September.

"You asked me about Foucault, petit. And I never gave
you an answer."

He paused. I held my breath, expecting another explosion.

"I should explain. I did know him, perhaps better than
many people ever did. We met once. But only once. It was
during a student uprising in the university at Vincennes,
where he taught philosophy. He never knew who I was. You
didn't bother with names and titles then. It was hard to tell
who was a student and who was a lecturer, if they were on
our side. I had already published *La Fuite*. And he was the
first person to comment on my work whose opinion I valued.
It's rare to find another man whose mind works through the
same codes, whose work is as anonymous, yet as personal
and lucid as your own. Especially a contemporary. It's more
usual to find the echo of your own voice in the past. You
are always listening, I think, when you write, for the voice
which answers. However oblique the reply may be. Foucault
never attempted to contact me. He did something more
frightening, provocative, profound. He wrote back, in his
published work. Many people have observed that our themes
are disturbingly similar, our styles of writing utterly different.
We read one another with the passion of lovers. Then we
began to write to one another, text for text. I went to all
his public lectures at the Collège de France. He saw me

there. He gave no sign. He was teaching in California when I was in America for the publication of *Midi*. I went to his seminars. There were over 170 people there. Once I was slightly late. He was standing silent at the lectern, looking at his notes, when I joined the crowd standing at the back of the hall. He looked up and we stared at one another. Then he began to speak. He never acknowledged me. He always knew when I was there.

"Our paths crossed frequently in Paris. We were often invited to the same events. We went to the same clubs, the same bars. We ignored each other's presence. We were careful to do that. Once, by chance, we were to be interviewed together for a programme about writing and homosexuality on France Culture. We both refused, giving the same reason. That we were happy to be interviewed alone but that we would not be drawn into discussion with the other. He was told of my refusal and apparently he laughed and laughed. His laugh was famous. The decision we made, to write to and for each other, was intimate and terrible. It was a secret that could never be shared. It was a strange hidden gesture of mutual consent. The disputes we had were oblique, subtle, contorted. No less passionate for that. His history of sexuality was like a challenge to me, a fist shaken. *L'Evadé* was to have been the first novel in a trilogy, a new departure for me. As he approached my austerity, my abstraction, I turned away towards a writing that was less perfect. I began to search for a style that would be brutal, aggressive, against serenity. I was sharpening my next set of demands, on him, on myself.

"He was the reader for whom I wrote."

Paul Michel gazed out into the blue void. I heard joyful shouting from the beach below. Paul Michel spoke again.

"He kept the secret. He never betrayed me."

I could restrain myself no longer.

"But it wasn't a secret. Anybody can see it. All that's necessary is to read you both. Side by side, page after page."

"I know. That's the joke. They talk of influence, threads, preoccupations. They know nothing about the unspoken pact. That was absolutely clear between us. We knew each other's secrets, weaknesses and fears, petit. The things that were hidden from the world. He wanted to write fiction. He fretted that he was not handsome. That the boys would not flock to him, court him. I lived that life for him, the life he envied and desired. I had no authority, no position. I was just a clever charismatic boy with the great gift of telling stories. He was always more famous than I was. He was the French cultural monument. I was never respectable. But I wrote for him, petit, only for him. The love between a writer and a reader is never celebrated. It can never be proved to exist. But he was the man I loved most. He was the reader for whom I wrote."

I was silent. I never told him that I had read his letters to Foucault. I think he knew that I had done.

The last day we went back to the beach was the thirtieth of September. We decided to drive north on that Friday and to take our time, stopping at Avignon or Orange so that we would be in Clermont by Sunday night. I decided to fight the next round in Sainte-Marie itself. I had made my decision, but I had said nothing to him. There was no question in my mind that I would ever return to England. Nothing in the whole world mattered more to me now than Paul Michel. That never changed. I can remember how naïve, how unsuspecting, how happy I was. I had won all the past battles, to find him, to set him free. I would win the next one. And the next. But I had never anticipated what he still had to say to me. He was particularly gentle with me all that day. I would turn to face him and find his grey eyes upon me, no longer hooded or cautious. There was no more disguise, no pretence. He was improvident with his love, indiscreet with his desire. I know that he was now telling me the truth, all the truth.

I hung my feet over the railings and watched the sand leak out of a hole in the toe of my gym shoes. I was aware of Paul Michel's now dark sunburnt arm balancing the back of my chair. We watched the windsurfers cutting across the slow swell in the warm wind. It was late afternoon and the beach had begun to fill with a gaggle of working people. Some arrived wearing their office clothes, negotiating the steps with their plastic bags and city shoes. For the first time, I noticed that the huge concrete blocks protecting the entrance to the port were all shaped like coffins. The mark of the cross in faint, eroded black paint was upon each one. But they were gigantic, over fifteen feet long, six feet wide, an uncanny momento mori converted into a break-water. I pointed them out to Paul Michel. He simply nodded.

"They've been there for years, petit. The harbour bar is built on a natural shelf of rock which the coffins are reinforc-ing. If you climb behind them there's a way down to a promontory on the rocks which has a wonderful sequence of pools. I used to sunbathe over there."

I turned to look at him, squinting in the bright light.

"So you know the beach? I didn't realise that you had been here before."

He smiled slightly.

"You're going a lovely colour." He stroked my back affec-tionately. "You're like a polished walnut table. So am I. You'll be able to sell me off as a restored antique."

We watched some children below filtering sand into bottles and then pushing them out to sea.

"Any messages in the bottles?" asked Paul Michel.

"I don't think so."

"Because if there are you must rush down and get them. That's what my writing was. Messages in bottles."

"And don't you have any more messages to send?"

"No."

I was silent for a moment. Then he went on as if I had spoken, asking and replying to his own question.

"And what is there left for a novelist to do when he has sent out all his messages? . . . Rien que mourir."

I sat up enraged.

"I wish you wouldn't fucking well talk like that. It gets on my nerves. You're not mad. Or doomed. You're getting well. You are well. You'll write again. Even better."

He looked at me, detached, amused. I felt like the bull, watching the pointed darts in the toreador's hands.

"Have you ever loved a woman, petit?"

I was caught off guard, and as always, both evaded the question and told the truth.

"I'd never loved a man before. Until I read you."

He smiled at the oddness of the verb in the context of our conversation.

"No? Well . . . I'm flattered. Let me tell you about something which happened to me. It has never ceased to haunt me. It was fifteen years ago. In August, around the time when you and I first came to the Midi. The beaches on the front were packed so I was looking for somewhere quieter to brood and to swim. I found an empty sheet of hot rock a long way away from everybody else. Out there, beyond the coffin breakwater. It was barren, empty, a sequence of sharp rocks and pools. I took notes, slept during the hottest part

of the day. I always travelled alone, lived alone. I've never
even shared a room with anyone else, not since childhood.
It's odd sometimes, hearing your breathing in the night,
when I don't sleep. You bring back the taste of my childhood,
petit. I chose solitude and the deeper dimensions of that
choice, which are inevitable and necessary. I condemned
myself to isolation and loneliness. It was the only way I
could work, it was my way of defending myself. I used to
write in complete silence. I used to spend time listening
to silence.

"Even here in the Midi I spent the days alone. But I had
spent only one day meditating, like Prometheus chained to
the rock, when my refuge was breached. I arrived early
in the morning to find a boy, pale-skinned, scrawny, curly-
haired, wearing nothing but jeans cut off to frayed shorts,
investigating the rock pools. We stared at one another, both
clearly resentful. He had already claimed that bank of rocks
for his kingdom and had set up a pattern of traps in the
pools, all of which were empty apart from a few weeds. We
re-set the nets and I made a few suggestions. He had huge
eyes, an owl-like glare. I was fascinated by the intensity
of this child, his halting French and his complete, staring
fearlessness.

"An odd friendship flared up between us. He spent the
morning playing in the rocks or diving for objects. He
brought me back whatever he found. I shared my salami,
bread and apples with him. He vanished in search of his
father at one o'clock, but came back later in the day to
check his traps again. I like the honesty, the knowingness
of children. He told me that he was nearly eleven years old,
that unsettling time of questioning, awakening. He asked
me what I was writing and spelt out whole sentences in my
notebook, with uncanny concentration, fighting for their

meanings. I remember him telling me how much he liked reading. Everything he had read sounded too adult for his age; strange, unsuitable texts, Zola, Flaubert, T. E. Lawrence, Oscar Wilde. He was pleased that we had read all the same things. I asked him which he had liked best of all the works he had read by Oscar Wilde. Unhesitating, he replied, 'The Picture of Dorian Gray.' Then he looked at me suspiciously. 'Not everyone who's beautiful is honest.'

"I tried very hard to keep a straight face. It would have been proof of my dishonesty if I had laughed.

"But I asked who gave him all his books. I discovered that he had no mother and that his father had never bought any books for children. He had simply let the child loose all along his shelves.

"He never told me his name. He never asked me mine.

"I began to hope that he would already be there when I climbed over the rocks in the mornings.

"He asked me why I was always alone. I told him that I was a writer. And that most writers worked alone. He asked me if I was a famous writer. I said that I was fairly famous and had won the Prix Goncourt. He asked if it was a very important prize and if I had a big house and gardens. I told him that I rented what used to be a servant's room in the roof of an hotel. And how I remember the way he screwed up his nose at this. And asked me why I lived like an impoverished hermit if I was in fact a rich man. I realised then that I had assumed all the clichés of austerity.

"And I remember his reply. He said, 'Why make do with the bare minimum? Why live on so little? If I were you I'd want everything. I wouldn't be satisfied with so little.'

"And I remember how strange this sounded, coming from the stillness of that bony, innocent face, the salt sticking to his short, wet curls. And I laughed and said, 'You mean I should have a big house and car and a wife and children?'

"His face clouded and aged with contempt. He took on the aspect of a dwarf and answered with devastating, terrible seriousness. 'No. I didn't mean that. Anybody can have all those. You should want—all of it. All this.' And he stretched out his arm, now reddening in the sun, high above his head, indicating the limitless, overarching blue above us, the forever retreating line of the sea, stretching away to Africa.

"I stared and laughed. He shook his finger at me like a goblin. Then recited the day's lesson with ecclesiastical solemnity. 'It seems to me that you live in a mean and lonely way. You should live on a grander scale. You should never put up with shit if you can get cake.'

"I was utterly charmed.

"And I know what you're thinking, petit. That I fell in love with this child who had read about buggery, castration, the class struggle, violent perverted sex and had come out upon the last page, still in possession of a breathtaking, romantic innocence and an arrogance that insisted on his own unflinching understanding of the world. You think that I'm telling you about first love. You're right. That boy was my first love. And I was his.

"He had his own ideas. He even had ideas about the kinds of books I should write. He looked at *La Maison d'Eté* and told me that it was far too short. I should aim at greater things.

" 'Huge ones. Much longer than the things you write now. They should be vast. Not perfect. Nothing's perfect. If you try to make it look perfect then it's only pretending.'

"I said that he was a literary megalomaniac. He didn't know the word. He made me spell it out and explain all its dimensions. He made me write it down. He asked me to tell him the story of *Midi*, which I was writing then. I think I made it more exciting in the re-telling. He asked me why the characters could never be happy, never united. I explained, without hesitation, and without thinking, that it was an allegory of homosexuality. It was then that he amazed me.

" 'What's an allegory?' he asked, 'and why should homo-sexuality always be unhappy in books? Elsewhere, it isn't.'

"I suggested that we should check the rock pools, and in his accusing stare I had the reprimand for my evasions.

"He never engaged in pointless games or aimless conversations. There was always a goal to be achieved or information to be gathered. I remembered this, the terrifying purposefulness of an only child. I had the same inability to waste time. Day after day we haunted the rocks, inspected the weed-covered crevasses and tunnels, swam in the clear, warm water. I remember once, watching the curve of his back as he sat squatting, peering into the lapping, breathing sea. And noticing the way in which each vertebra was separate, a long bony chain, fragile, yet indestructible. He was extraordinarily strong.

"Yes, I suppose I did fall in love with that child. But there was something more important. We became friends. What equality is possible between a child of eleven and a man in his thirties? Friendship, complicity, trust make all things equal. You remind me of him.

"But it was only a matter of time before the father came in search of the vanishing child. Parents rightly suspect that the serpents of corruption are lurking on every street corner. Or in this case stretched out upon the summer rocks.

"The scene he witnessed was tranquil and innocent enough. We were playing cards and drinking Badoit under the shadow of a huge grey rock, an overhanging mass like the nose of an elephant. Then the father was suddenly present, making the third in the triangle, standing above us. He was wearing jeans and a light, cream jacket. I was aware of the coloured outline, as if he had been one of the child's draw-ings. I think I expected him to pull out a gun. The child looked up briefly. Then concentrated on his cards.

" 'This is my Dad,' was all he said.

"The father crouched beside us and looked at our cards.

" 'Twist. You've got to,' he said to the boy, covering his eyes from the sun. He was about ten years older than I, slick, good-looking. I noticed a gold signet ring on the last finger of his left hand. We played out the game. The child won.

" 'I hope you weren't cheating,' his father said casually.

" 'I never cheat unless I have to,' was the reply. Then the father addressed me directly.

" 'Will you have dinner with us tonight? We go on to Italy tomorrow.' We looked straight at one another. I agreed. And at the same moment I realised that he was homosexual.

"They were staying at the best hotel in Nice. The moment of reversal, of revelation if you like, came that night on the steps of the hotel. The child was waiting for me, perched on the balustrade beside a huge palm tree in a Roman urn. He was on the lookout, alert and tense as a cat. But I saw him first, and noticed the brushed curls, washed with gold, the cheekbones pink with sunburn and freckles, the long arms curled around the knees. His ambiguity suddenly broke over me with all the force of the sea against the great rocks. I had not mistaken the nature of this child. But I had certainly been deceived in her sex. She swung down from the solitary ledge and rushed into my arms.

"When we parted that night she said something I shall never forget. Largely because only children, children like myself, children like that girl, always keep their promises.

She said, 'If you love someone—you know where they are
and what has happened to them. And you put yourself at
risk to save them if you can. If you get into trouble I promise
that I'll come to save you.'

"I think that's the strangest, most romantic declaration
I've ever had.

" 'Will you?' I said.

" 'Yes, and when I can read French better I will read every
word you write. I will be your reader.'

"Wasn't that an extraordinary promise petit? They were
English. Her father was a charming man. He worked in the
Bank of England. I sometimes wonder if she remembers me."

I sat staring at Paul Michel, speechless and terribly frightened. Then I said, "She never forgot you. She kept her
promise. She sent me."

He didn't reply for a moment. It was now after seven
o'clock and the light was softening on the barrels, the rocks,
the ropes, supporting the café above the beach. The world
was being transformed into luminous gold.

"Oh? Did she?" was all he said.

That night he was restless again. I was almost asleep when
I heard him getting out of bed.

"What's the matter?"

"Shhh, petit. I'm just going downstairs for a drink."

He kissed my ear and stroked my head for a moment. I
fell fast asleep again.

It was after four in the morning when I heard an urgent
tapping on my door. I sat up shaking. Paul Michel had not
returned. I was alone. It was a woman's voice at the door.
Through a fog of sleep and fear I recognised Marie-France
Legras. She was calling my name. But she didn't wait for me
to reply, she was already in the room, calling and calling.

"What is it?" I stammered.

"The police are here."

"Paul Michel?"

"I'm afraid it's bad news."

I howled out his name and began to cry uncontrollably. I had been waiting for this, the empty bed, the call in the night. I had known that he would not wait for me. Marie-France put her arms around me and whispered all the gentle reassuring things that she would have said to her son. I realised that she was crying too. It was some hours before I was able to face the police.

The manner of his dying was bizarre. He had taken the car, although he was not authorised to drive, and had set out along the coast road of the Esterel in the direction of Cannes. You can't build up much speed on that road, even in a more powerful car than a 2CV, it is too narrow, uneven, winding. There wasn't much traffic. A gigantic white owl, drawn to the yellow lights and the swerving car, fixed its great eyes on his face and plummeted towards the Citroën. The creature smashed through the windscreen, sinking its claws into his face and throat. The car hurtled into the cliff. He was killed instantly. They laid him out on the stretcher with the great dead bird wrapped around his face. Weeks later the inquest gave the cause of death as multiple injuries received on impact; accidental death, killed in a car accident, a futile death, daily, banal. But the autopsy revealed that he had enough alcohol and paracetamol mixed in his blood to end the days of several Hollywood film stars. He had taken all the drugs in our bathroom cabinet, everything, even the travel sickness tablets and swallowed them down with a bottle of whisky. It had been a miracle that he had been able to drive as far as he did. There had been no mistake. He had intended to die. He had been searching for the great white owl on the narrow frontier between the mountains and the sea.

And then I knew what he had seen—the last vision he had had before the darkness had been drawn across his sight: the belly of a great white owl, its wings outstretched, lit from beneath, its huge yellow eyes, the pupils sharpening to slits as his claws reached for the glass and the white face beyond, blurred and magnified, as if by a powerful lens.

Marie-France went out to FNAC and bought all his books.

"I don't read much usually. And certainly not this sort of thing. I like historical fiction. But I feel that we owe it to him. They said that Le Seuil are bringing out a new compact edition with all his political essays. I think I'll just read the novels."

The police interviewed me for hours. I kept breaking down and crying like a child. They poured bottles of Evian down my throat. The gendarme at the typewriter corrected my French. He had to look up how to spell schizophrenia in the dictionary.

Early on the morning of the second day I had a phone call. A very careful English accent puzzled me at first.

"Hello? Is that you? This is Dr Jacques Martel. Your London friends rang me in Paris. The police rang the hospital too. So I've come from Sainte-Anne and on behalf of Paul Michel's father. He's too ill and senile to understand that his son is dead . . . I'm at the airport . . . Don't worry, I'll take a taxi. I'm here to help you with the paperwork . . . Yes . . . you won't believe the bureaucracy. And we have to move fairly fast. They'll release the body at the end of next week."

"Do you have the necessary authorisation?" I gulped helplessly. "They told me I didn't."

"I should think I do. I'm Paul Michel's legal representative. I'll be with you in an hour or so."

I sat down beside the phone, my body tingling with shock and fear. There were too many pieces of this story that I had not seen, too many connections that had never been revealed. The man with the wolf's smile and the sharpened teeth had been the hermit in the cave, warning me of the dangers ahead. I had been watched and guided, every step of the way. I was their Red Cross Knight, sent out to find the soul that was lost. I had never understood the nature and meaning of my task and now I had been defeated. I was still sitting on the floor beside the phone when I heard Baloo howling at the iron gates. Jacques Martel, in a light suit, his jacket over his arm, his briefcase and travelling bag in the other hand, stood, erect and unflinching as a mountain pine, on the other side of the white bars.

I thrust my face against the cold gate.

"Why didn't you tell me when we first met?" I was almost shouting.

"I told you all you needed to know." His manner was cool, utterly assured.

I thought of my Germanist, her mass of curly hair and intense, owl-like gaze. I felt imprisoned by conspiracy.

"Did she know too? Was she in on it? Are you all a part of this?"

Baloo howled at the blue sky.

"Ask her." Jacques Martel stepped calmly through the gate and the dog began to circle his legs, sniffing.

"Don't be afraid." He gave me his travelling bag and took my arm with professional firmness. "I'm here now. I'm here to take care of you."

I gazed up at him, now utterly terrified. What happened to the people who were consigned to his care? But it was so easy to silence me, to deflect my hysteria. Marie-France kept saying, you're ill, you've had a terrible shock, you've lost your friend. I was taken to the doctor. I couldn't stop crying. They gave me tranquillisers and I began to see the bright, cooling world through a blur. I hardly ate. I slept for ten hours a day. Jacques Martel took charge of everything. I remember his hands, white, smooth, untouched by work, taking the fountain pen out of his inside breast pocket, signing all the necessary papers, lifting the phone, filling in the forms. I fought against numbness, and torrents of tears.

"You must eat. Here's some vegetable soup. Do try. It's very nourishing." Marie-France smothered me with motherly concern. Her husband retired to his newly built furnace and spent the evenings devising ever more elaborate and sinister pizzas with exotic fillings.

The funeral was fixed for the twelfth of October. Jacques Martel decided to bury him with his mother in the village churchyard above the vines near Gaillac, outside Toulouse. We were then confronted by extraordinary administrative questions, Gothic and bizarre. Were we to hire a hearse and drive to Toulouse? Was cremation in Nice a preferable option? So that we could drive him back ourselves, carrying only an urn in the boot of the car? Should we have the body flown in and engage to have the local undertakers meet us at the airport? Jacques Martel studied all the options.

Articles, reviews, retrospectives on his work began to appear in the press. Marie-France defended me against the journalists. Baloo guarded the gates. In any case I had nothing to say. In the evening, six days after his death, I phoned the Germanist at her flat in Maid's Causeway. I was at a loss and utterly defeated. I couldn't ask my parents to

come. I couldn't go through with it alone. I felt that I had
no one left.

"Hello," she said crisply.

"It's me."

She paused. Then she said, "I've told your supervisor you'll
be late back and I've left a note in College."

"Oh, thanks."

She guessed at once what I was unable to ask.

"Do you want me to come?"

I started crying into the mouthpiece of the telephone.

"Don't cry," she said, and I could hear the snap of her
cigarette lighter close to the phone.

She agreed to abandon Schiller for a week or so and sent
a telegram with no information other than her flight number.

BA 604. *Arrives Nice 18.30 tomorrow.*

I was waiting in the great domed concourse among the
dogs and the security guards, still dressed in the same stained
T-shirt, jeans and gym shoes I had been wearing when he
told me the story of the boy on the beach. I stared at her
curls and glasses as she appeared from behind the barrier, as
if I was seeing her for the first time.

She arrived, fresh, brisk, knowing, bearing all the chill of
England. She kissed me. Then she made a more careful
second inspection.

"You look awful," she said.

"I know."

"Well, you've been through it, I see." But she didn't
specify what it was that I had so unsuccessfully traversed.
She carried her own bag. She more or less carried me. I was
swept out on to the pavement and into the early autumn
heat. The light was changing. Now the air was vast, huge,
expanding all around us. She summoned a taxi.

"We could go by bus," I suggested.

"Don't be ridiculous. You couldn't stand the journey."

She was right. I leaned against her and cried all the way back into the city. Jacques Martel was delighted to see her. From then on they took all the decisions together.

It proved to be prohibitively expensive to fly the body back to Toulouse. For some reason a corpse's ticket costs a good deal more than that of a living person. So we decided to drive in convoy back to Gaillac. His aunt, now eighty, still clear-headed, was his inheritor. She was busy arranging the funeral and had decided that the returning sinner should receive a decent Catholic burial, but with the minimum of expense. She put one announcement in the local papers. But it was in all the national press. The curé had been primed and given strict orders to be exceedingly discreet. Journalists and cameras were banned. She told Jacques Martel that she was very relieved that it had been a road accident and not AIDS. He was righteously furious, but kept his temper on the phone. Madame Legras said that it was no use quarrelling with people like his aunt who might be incredibly wealthy, but were still peasants, and who had almost certainly never read any of his books. I didn't remind her that, until the previous week, she hadn't either.

It was decided, without any discussion, that I should not be present at the "levée du corps". The Germanist took me to an exhibition of Picasso's engravings instead. For the rest of my life I shall remember those elongated satyrs playing Pan pipes, and the evil expressions of the Minotaurs. We didn't know what to do with the few things he had left in the room. I packed up all his belongings with mine, and took them with me on my journey home.

I hadn't quite bargained for the fact that we were taking the motorway. In Britain the hearse usually proceeds at a walking pace. But we hurtled through the bright, autumn light down the fast lane. The great jagged red mountains of the Midi rushed past, the pink folds of Mont Ste-Victoire dropped behind us. We sat in a traffic jam outside Arles and I stared at the back of the van in which his coffin was securely wedged. It could have been a police van taking someone to jail, or a bullion haul in disguise. We even paused for lunch at a service station and left Paul Michel quietly parked under the fragrant umbrella pines. We were all very sober, very quiet. I kept feeling sick. The Germanist never let go of my hand. And I was grateful for that.

The journey took us all day. We got to Gaillac just as the light was fading on the hills behind Toulouse. The van disappeared, leaving me with a sinking sensation of panic and loss. As long as I knew he was travelling with us I was obscurely comforted. Jacques Martel bundled us into the Hôtel des Voyagers, just off the square in Gaillac.

"Where will they put him?" I demanded.

"In the church."

"With no one there? In the dark?"

Jacques Martel stared at me.

"There are always candles," he said.

I wanted to spend the night in the church. Jacques Martel shrugged his shoulders and walked out of our room. The Germanist sat smoking, crosslegged on our bed.

"I wouldn't advise it," she said. "You'll get too tired and upset. And we have to get our flowers first thing in the morning. Then we can take them to the church and wait if you like. But you ought to pay your respects to the aunt. And you want to be on form for that. Also, I've got something to show you."

I sat disconsolate, my head in my hands. Then I asked her, "What have you got to show me?"

She had written a letter to Paul Michel which she proposed to sellotape to the coffin along with our roses.

"They usually take all the flowers off and then put them
on the grave afterwards. So we've just got to insist that they
bury the roses. That's why you've got to charm the wicked
aunt. She has every reason to be grateful to you after all . . ."
She had it all planned.

The letter was already sealed.

"Here you are. Here's a copy. It's from you. So it's important that you know what you've said."

"But I didn't write it."

"Doesn't matter. Pretend you did. It will say what you
wanted to say to him."

I read the letter.

Cher Maître,

I was your reader too. He was not your only reader. You
had no right to abandon me. Now you leave me in the
same chasm which you faced when you lost the reader you
loved best of all. You were privileged, spoiled; not every
writer knows that his reader is there. Your writing is a hand
stretched out in the dark, into an unknowing void. Most
writers have no more than that. And yet how can I reproach
you? You still wrote for me.

You gave me what every writer gives the reader he loves—
trouble and pleasure. There were always two dimensions
to our friendship. We knew one another, played together,
talked together, ate together. It was painfully hard to leave
you. What I miss most are your hands and your voice. So
often we would be watching something else and discussing
what we saw. I loved that; your cold gaze upon the world.
But the more intimate relationship we had was the one
you constructed when you were writing for me. I followed

you, across page after page after page. I wrote back in the margins of your books, on the flyleaf, on the title page. You were never alone, never forgotten, never abandoned. I was here, reading, waiting.

This is my first and last letter to you. But I will never abandon you. I will go on being your reader. I will go on remembering you. I will go on writing within the original shapes you made for me. You said that the love between a writer and a reader is never celebrated, can never be proven to exist. That's not true. I came back to find you. And when I had found you I never gave you up. Nor will I do so now. You asked me what I feared most. I never feared losing you. Because I will never let you go. You will always have all my attention, all my love. Je te donne ma parole. I give you my word.

"Well?"

Behind her glasses she was no longer quite so confident that she had done the right thing. But she had written the truth. It was so simply told. I had loved him terribly. And now he was dead. I clutched her shoulders and howled.

"He'll never read this. He's dead. He's dead. He's dead."

She rocked me in her arms for a while. Then she said fiercely, "How do you know he'll never read it?"

There was no answer to that.

Next morning she went out with her credit card and bought 480 francs worth of roses. The letter was wound round the stalks, fastened with string and hidden inside a huge mass of accompanying foliage. Jacques Martel drove us out to the house. Suddenly I knew that I would recognise the gates, the long lines of poplars, already turning; that I would remember the house with its narrow brickwork and symmetrical row of lozenge windows under the receding dogtooth of the corniche, beneath gutterless eaves. I would already know the long lines of vines and their changing colours. His memories had become mine. I would look up to the red walls of the cemetery on the hill, recognise the worn grey cross on the family mausoleum, occupying the highest point in the graveyard. I would know the place to which we were carrying him to lie down at last and forever alongside his mother and the man whose name he bore, the man he had called grandfather, Jean-Baptiste Michel.

His aunt was small, bent double with rheumatism, and very suspicious. She stood among the remains of the Michel family inheritance, huge old sideboards, cupboards, dressers, a cheap battered armchair with hideous nylon cushions, poised before the vast opaque screen of the television. Her face was shut and mean. She wore black. She stared up at us for longer than anyone could possibly consider polite. Then she shook my hand grudgingly and did not ask us to sit down. Instead she rummaged for her coat, her keys. Every door was carefully locked before we left the house by the back gate and took the path across the fields to the church. I followed Paul Michel back into the past. I retraced his steps.

It was a clear, fresh day with a bright wind. The tiny church was small and dark, filled with flowers. We were nearly an hour in advance of the funeral, but the undertakers were already there, slick as gangsters in dark glasses and black gloves. So were many cars, almost all of them with Paris registration plates. I shook hands with people I had never seen before. They were all young. I had not even taken in the coffin before we entered the church. It was a rich walnut brown, the colour of his sunburn, with ornate, silver handles. The thing was covered in flowers.

The Germanist went into action. She took one careful

measure of the aunt then bypassed her completely and addressed herself solely to the undertakers. I saw her whispering to the ghoul in charge. He gathered up the roses, bowed to the altar with the flowers in his arms, and then quietly re-arranged the entire coffin so that the roses covered the plaque across Paul Michel's chest. I had great difficulty imagining him inside. It was as if he had been locked up permanently indoors.

She slid back into the pew beside me and put her mouth to my ear. The church around her was filling up.

"It's OK. I've fixed it. They'll bury the roses with him. I gave them 200 francs."

She was ingenious, but without shame.

I can't remember much about the service. I couldn't follow what the priest said. He talked about the family and how creative Paul Michel had been and listed his numerous services to French culture. He talked about his tragically early death and never mentioned the fact that he was homosexual or that he had been locked up in an asylum. His version of Paul Michel sounded unlikely and inconsistent. But I was too distressed to care. I did notice, however, the words of the hymn he had chosen.

Et tous ceux qui demeurent dans l'angoisse
ou déprimés, accablés par leurs fautes,
Le Seigneur les guérit, leur donne vie,
leur envoie son pardon et sa parole.

And I clutched at this because it was the last promise that the Germanist had made to him. I give you my word. When the moment came to say goodbye and each person present scattered holy water on the flowers covering his coffin I realised that there were more people waiting outside

the church than could enter in. The march past was without
end. There were some couples, women and men together,
but most of them were men.

We climbed the hill to the graveyard, the entire procession disorganised, colourful, chaotic. I was crying silently,
streams of tears, unstopping, a huge, formless grief wrapped
its arms about me. The Germanist held me fiercely round
the waist, but her eyes never left the roses, bobbing ahead
on the shoulders of six gasping undertakers, who were finding
the hill harder to negotiate than they had expected. We
couldn't all fit into the graveyard. I looked back. In the
October morning sun, stretching back down the hill, was a
long, straggling line of pilgrims, following Paul Michel.

If you come from a wealthy family you are not buried in
earth. A huge granite slab had been prised off the family
vault. He was to be encased forever in concrete. They rest
one coffin on top of another. Eventually they rot down. I
clutched her hand. Unfortunately we were at the head of
the procession and could see perfectly well what was happen-
ing. The priest began the chant. His words vanished into
the wind. Every so often all the people around me intoned,
"Pour toi, Seigneur . . ." I was aware of the old aunt's tuneless
whistle. But they all seemed to know what to sing. The
coffin rocked against the mossy concrete walls with a grating
clank as the ropes were lowered. The men had very little
space in which to move. The graves pressed against one
another. I could see a dark shape, sinister, fresh, waiting at
the bottom. They were there, one on top of the other, his
mother, his grandfather, his whispering grandmother, and
Paul Michel.

"There's no grave, no real grave, no earth," I hissed,
desperate.

"It's OK," she said quietly. "He liked cities. It's just more concrete. And the roses will last longer."

He was right about her intensity, her sense of purpose and her complete fearlessness. I realised then why he had been so drawn to the boy on the beach. They were two of a kind, watching the world with cold eyes.

We walked back to the house through a multitude of sombre, concentrated disciples. A gang of smokers cowered under the cemetery wall. Jacques Martel had the aunt on his arm and the priest marched before us. The undertakers, like Caesar's soldiers, stood guard around the tomb. The throng parted before us. I saw nothing but a blur of faces. We were treated as family. The aunt pulled Jacques' face down towards her.

"Who are all these people?" she demanded.

But it was the Germanist who replied. She materialised on the other side of Madame Michel.

"They're his readers," she said.

Madame Michel glared at the mass with undisguised mistrust. Her erring nephew had earned a lot of good money and bad publicity. She was neither fooled nor convinced.

We flew back to London from Toulouse on the following day. I had missed one week of full term. The Germanist had simply said that I was ill so everyone sympathised with my shattered state, which was attributed to viral flu and food poisoning.

In the weeks that followed I told the Germanist everything. I needed to talk. But there was one passage in the story that I never told: Paul Michel's encounter with the boy on the beach. I never told this story because it was her secret, the secret pact she had with him. But I read and re-read her letter to Paul Michel. I now understood the code.

The letter could have been written by either one of us. She had kept her word. It was now up to me to keep mine.

I wrote my thesis much along the lines I had originally planned. I did not include a biographical section. I never even told my supervisor that I had known Paul Michel. I gave nothing away in my acknowledgements. That summer was like a paving stone torn out of my life, a blank square. I told my parents, of course. They were a little shocked that I had got so closely involved with someone who was clearly unstable and whom they had never met. Once again, they asked to meet the Germanist. I begged her to come home with me. She refused, and told me, with unnecessary aggression, never to ask her again.

In the years that followed I held a Junior Research Fellowship at my old college and won the Foucault Travel Prize. I spent the money travelling in America. Eventually I got a job in the French department at one of the London colleges. And I used to lecture on Paul Michel. The Germanist went to work in the Goethe-Schiller Archive in Weimar. We wrote to each other for a year or so. Then I lost touch. Sometimes I see the titles of articles she's published in the *Year's Work in German Studies*. Someone once told me that she was writing a biography of Schiller and bringing out a new edition of the Goethe-Schiller *Briefwechsel*. No doubt I shall buy a copy when it appears in the catalogues.

I try not to think about him. I simply work on the texts. But there is an evil dream which comes back to me, which recurs again and again. The detail of my dream has a hallucinatory intensity, which I cannot shake off. It is winter and the maize fields have been cut. All that is left are the rough lines of yellow, brittle stalks, thick and difficult to negotiate. I am stumbling across a huge, desolate field where the remains of the crop are burning. It is bitterly cold. The fires across the stubble burn unevenly, some patches are simply smoking black ashes, some are untouched, rigid with frost, but elsewhere the wind carries the flame on down the row, through the crackling dry ranks of trampled, discarded corn. Far away at the rim of the field I see a long line of bare poplars and the sky behind, a pale, luminous, chill cream. Then through the smoke and the scattered fires I see Paul Michel standing, watching me. He does not move. It is bitterly cold. He is not wearing a coat or gloves, his shirt is open at the throat. He stands amid the fires, watching me. He neither moves nor speaks. It is bitterly cold. I never saw him in winter. I knew him for a single season. I stumble on towards him and I never come closer. Then I see that there is someone else present in the field. The shape of a man, a long way off, behind Paul Michel, glimmers through the smoke of the stubble fires. I cannot make him out. I do not know who he is. The scene freezes before me like a painting I can never enter, a scene whose meaning remains unreachable, obscure.

I always wake shivering, wretched, alone.

Paul MICHEL	Michel FOUCAULT
b. 15 June 1947	b. 15 October 1926
Toulouse	Poitiers
Educated Collège St Bénédict	Educated Collège St Stanislaus
1966–70 Ecole des Beaux-Arts. Studied painting and sculpture	1946 Ecole Normale Supérieure
1968 *La Fuite* trans. UK/USA *Escape* 1970	1948 First suicide attempt

1974 *Ne demande pas:*
   roman trans. UK/USA
   Don't Ask
1976 *La Maison d'Eté.* Prix
   Goncourt. trans. UK
   The Summer House
1980 Midi: *roman*

1983 *L'Evadé: roman* trans
   USA *The Prisoner Escapes*
Diagnosed schizophrenic:
   sectioned Hôpital Ste-
   Anne, Paris. June 1984

Killed in a road accident,
   Nice. 30 September
   1993
Buried Gaillac

1961 *Madness and*
   Civilization

1966 *The Order of Things*

1969 *Archaeology of*
   Knowledge
1975 *Discipline and*
   Punishment
1976 *A History of Sexuality*

1984 *The Care of the Self,*
   The Uses of Pleasure

Died of AIDS, Paris. 26
   June 1984

Buried Poitiers